Jimgrim and
the Woman Ayisha

Jimgrim and the Woman Ayisha

Talbot Mundy

WILDSIDE PRESS

JIMGRIM AND THE WOMAN AYISHA

Published by
Wildside Press, LLC
www.wildsidepress.com

CHAPTER I

"Ali, I say I go with him!"

CONSIDER the situation for a moment first. There were twenty of us — seventeen Arabs, Narayan Singh the Sikh, myself, and Grim. We were in Petra over-Jordan, which was no-man's land until Ali Higg, self-styled Lion of Petra, friend of the Prophet of Islam, Lord of the Limits of the Desert and Lord of the Waters — Ali Higg the Terrible, swooped into it from Arabia, and with the aid of Jael, his European wife, established himself there as a thorn in the flank of Palestine.

You couldn't choose a better place to be a thorn in. Impregnable without long-range artillery; inaccessible except by aeroplanes, if once the Valley of Moses leading into it through a twelve-foot gap were blocked; furnished with enough half-ruined graves and temples for accommodation purposes; close enough to Palestine for sudden raids, and surrounded by dry desert over which no mandatory power would think of sending an army if that could possibly be helped, Petra is the perfect outlaw's paradise — a paradise of opal set in savage mountains.

As for ourselves, you could hardly call us an official expedition, nor even exactly authorized, for Grim enjoyed a free hand, subject to the definite proviso that he would be promptly disowned by the Palestine authorities if trouble came of it. The British, having heard from the tax-payer, did not want to send an army against Ali Higg, besides which they had no mandate yet for the trans-Jordan country, as Ali Higg and all the Bedouins were well aware.

An American, even though commissioned in the British army, can get away with things no Britisher would dare attempt because, of course, the authorities would have to stand behind a Britisher, whereas Americans are all born crazy and act without authority, and everybody knows it, and there you are, old top; so what's the use? And Grim by using brains and information, which is a combination nobody can beat, had cornered Ali Higg, as I told in the last story. One hundred and forty of Ali's men, under a veteran named Ibrahim ben Ah, were resting their camels miles away in an oasis. The remaining forty and odd were camped in another direction.

Jael, Ali Higg's wife, after being made prisoner, had grudgingly agreed to help Grim tame her lord and master; and what with drenching him thoroughly, lancing his boils and catching him at an all-around disadvantage, we had forced him to give a hostage for good behavior in the shape of a deposit of fifty thousand pounds lying in his wife's name in the Bank of Egypt.

So far, good; but there were complications. In the first place, that document was not worth a plugged piastre until safely under lock and key in Jerusalem; for Ali Higg would surely steal it back if he could. The money had been paid into the bank in gold, mainly half-sovereigns that were earned by Arab troops in the war against the Turks. The man who could squeeze all that money out of fighting Bedouins was unlikely to lose his grip on it, even for the three-year term of the agreement, if force or chicanery should provide him an alternative. If those troops of his should suddenly return, for instance, not only the agreement but our lives would be at stake.

The easiest course would have been to scoot out of Petra and head for Palestine, avoiding that oasis where the "army" waited. But Grim had made a promise, which prevented that. In return for Ali Higg's pledge and in the general interest of peace he had undertaken to deal with a sheikh at Abu Lissan, farther south, who with eight hundred men proposed to come and "eat up" the terrible Ali and his scant ten score.

While on our way southward there would be nothing to prevent Ali Higg from swooping on us treacherously from behind; but in dealing with people who might perhaps break faith there is nothing nearly so important as observing your own promises.

Nor was that all. Our opportunity to visit Petra, give the slip to Ali Higg's men, capture his head wife and corner the gentleman himself had come through Ayisha, his second wife, whom Grim had found making purchases in Hebron and who welcomed our escort on her way home across the desert. On the way she had fallen in love with Grim after the desperately swift fashion of the country. Thinking to poison Ali Higg, she had given him croton oil, which we provided. It served our purpose famously, but rather naturally maddened the fierce polygamist, who divorced her on the spot. So we had Ayisha on our hands, for we couldn't decently leave her to take the consequences.

When I was a boy at school I once borrowed from another boy a dime manual entitled "What To Do with a Dead Policeman." But that problem — solved, I remember, clumsily — was a very simple one compared to what we had to face.

Ayisha was a beautiful young woman, wholly bereft of convention in the Western sense, and totally resolved to win Grim for her own or know the reason why. Our rank and file, excepting Narayan Singh and myself, were all profound polygamists from El-Kalil, thieves by profession and conviction, and inclined to treat Ayisha's love affair as a prodigious joke; which, of course, it was, but for the infernal danger.

In fact, the whole situation was a joke, if you could only bring yourself to look at it in that way. What else could you call the intention of twenty men (not one an Englishman) cut off from supplies and support, to interfere between the warring tribes of North Arabia and breed peace in the process where none had ever been since history was written?

As I sat with my back against the wall of Ali Higg's cave overlooking the gorge of the City of Ghosts (as they call Petra) I tried to figure on our chances, but could meld nothing. Not that we weren't a pretty resourceful crew of a sort, and fit to fight, perhaps, three times our number; but the odds seemed overwhelming in that land where, as they say, "in the desert all men are enemies."

There wasn't one of us who could not mount his camel on the run, with a rifle in one hand, and our camels were the finest beasts that ever swung leg out of Syria. There was nothing about desert work that you could teach Grim or any of our seventeen Arabs. Narayan Singh was a Sikh in a thousand — a bold soldier of the old school, who should have been born a hundred years ago. As for myself, although comparatively new to Arabs and Arabia, I have prospected and hunted big game for a living up and down the length of Africa; and if diplomacy is not my long suit, I can endure; and physical strength has advantages.

But I laughed to myself as I sat there and looked at Grim, wondering at the freak of fortune that had thrown us together. True, I have chosen to spend my life looking for adventure where it grows; but a man likes to pile up a few dollars against old age and I have generally reckoned up the prospects in advance.

There was no money to be made in Grim's company. It didn't matter, as it happened, for I have not had more than my share of disappointment and need never starve again as long as the U. S. keeps a Government in being. But middle-aged dogs don't learn new tricks too easily, and I have known less surprising things than to find myself risking a sun-burned neck behind a whole-souled altruist without the remotest possibility of making a profit.

But you couldn't resist Grim. The man is like a lodestone, if you have the iron of adventure in you. I could take two of him, one in each hand, and shake them as a dog does rats; for though he is tall he is lightly framed, whereas the muscle stands on me in lumps. But when it comes to a call for those qualities that have always seemed to me man's finest, he can leave me standing still.

Mind you, I yield to no man in determination to live so according to the rules, as I understand them, that I can afford to look any man in the eye and tell him to go to Hell if I see fit. But that is one thing — comfortable in its way, and good for friendship. Genius is another. Grim has genius, besides a flair for leaving this old battered world a wee mite better than he found it.

I never heard him preach. Intimate friend of mine though he now is, I have hardly ever heard him discuss his principles. But I did hear him tell Jael Higg, by way of convincing her that her only possible course was to help him tame her ambitious lord if she hoped to escape imprisonment and deportation, that his one asset is understanding of Arabs and Arabia; that he is Hell bent, as he put it, on doing his bit in the world; and that his notion of a good big bit is to help Arabia to independence by preventing brigandage and civil war.

He clings to his American citizenship as some men stick to religion. The British made him a major on those terms because they needed him, and he accepted because it seemed the best way to carry on what he had in view. He is punctiliously loyal to the crowd whose uniform he wears occasionally, yet I never knew a man more outspoken to his paymasters whenever he disagrees with them, nor any one who took more liberties with orders.

His one annoying quality is that of keeping his thoughts to himself, hardly ever discussing a plan until it is perfect in his own mind and then telling you, perhaps, not more than half of it; after which he springs the rest on you as a surprise. But if you want to be friends with any man on earth you'll find there's something or other to put up with.

We all have our hobbies, even those who imagine they have none and boast of it. Having traveled widely I have had to make mine portable, and the two things that have increasingly obsessed me are the ancient history of whatever land I happen to be in, and the study of men's faces.

I had time to study two now — Grim's and Ali Higg's, for they were sitting face to face in the middle of the cave, Grim stooping from the shoulders as he squatted Arab fashion in exactly the same way that the robber chieftain did.

You would never have guessed that Grim wasn't an Arab, born in that part of Arabia. Unless in the secret, you would never have believed the two were not blood-brothers — possibly even twins. Seen in the comparative gloom of the cave they resembled a man facing his reflection.

Except for the bandages on Ali Higg's neck they were dressed alike, and the only difference noticeable at the first glance was the color of their eyes: Ali Higg's were brown and blood-shot; Grim's were keen and baffling — somewhere in the region of blue-gray. I have looked straight into them and not been able to tell their color.

Now the puzzling thing was this: That whereas every line of Grim's face made for strength, independence, honesty and all those other qualities that you recognize in a man at the first glance and like immediately, almost identical features made a rogue of Ali Higg. I believe you could have taken a pair of calipers and measured them without finding enough difference to split a hair about.

Both were clean-shaven, although Ali Higg's sparse whiskers had about two days' growth, which darkened and slightly changed the outline of his face. Both had that kind of chin with the suggestion of a cleft in it that usually goes along with a deep understanding of human nature.

Each man's eyes were large and seated rather deep. Each had a calm forehead, not much wrinkled, and their noses might have been cast from one mold — good, big noses, delicately curved along the bridge, with nostrils of the shape supposed to show good breeding.

They were the same height, and I don't believe either man weighed more than a hundred and forty pounds. I weigh nearly a hundred more than either of them. So does Narayan Singh.

Being dressed as an Indian Moslem from Lahore, with a great brown Bedouin cloak thrown over all, with my head showing shaved under the turban and a week's growth of nearly black beard sprouting, my disguise was pretty nearly perfect; but I dare bet that if a stranger could have entered that cave suddenly, he would have recognized Grim without hesitation as the man to reckon with; Ali Higg as the villain of the piece; Narayan Singh as a somewhat quarrelsome though loyal subordinate, and me as the looker-on.

It's difficult to see yourself as others might, but I expect that air of more or less detachment is hard to disguise when you have no real stake in a venture, except, of course, your life — something we most of us risk more casually than our money.

ALI HIGG watched us with similar curiosity, glancing from one to the other furtively, whereas Grim never shifted his gaze, but eyed the bandit steadily. It is one of the privileges of the East to sit as long as you want to and say nothing; outside on the ledge sat our old friend, Ali Baba with his sixteen sons and grandsons, overlooking the valley like vultures in a row; and nothing was likely to escape their eagle eyes, well fed though they were, and perhaps sleepy after gorging the bandit's rice and mutton. We had no need to seem in a hurry, and it was Ali Higg at last who spoke first.

"O Jimgrim, you have promised you will deal with that dog Hassan Saoud of Abu Lissan."

"True, O Lion of Petra."

"Then either you made that promise in order to trick me into signing an agreement; or else you are a madman! For how shall you, who have but nineteen men, get the better of Hassan Saoud, who styles himself the Avenger and has at least eight hundred?"

"Did I have the better of you?" Grim asked him.

"Father of ruses, yes! But you must give me back that agreement unless you keep your promise by smiting the Avenger. And how shall you do it?"

"Have I smitten you?" asked Grim.

The robber put some oily seeds into his mouth and chewed the cud on that for several minutes.

"But unless he is destroyed the Avenger will come and make war on me. If he wins, he will slay me and make some of my men prisoners, adding them to the force he has already.

"Thus you will have a more difficult man to deal with than I have been. Whereas I have only raided into Palestine a dozen times, he will make a holy war and plunder Jerusalem itself. So you must smite him or return me that agreement."

Grim laughed.

"You'd better help me then! If I fail, you'll suffer sooner than any one."

"Uh-uh!" the robber grunted. "Here in Petra I might defeat him, for the pass is narrow and a woman is the equal of a man. Out in the open I can not prevail against his numbers."

It was Grim's turn to sit silent. I was growing used to his masked changes of expression and did not doubt he knew what he was going to say; but I believe he turns over a sentence in his mind a dozen times before he uses it, on occasions when most men would seek to make an impression by rhetoric.

"They say I look like you," he said at last.

"They speak truly. We might have had one mother. Therefore it is unseemly that you should force a written pledge from me! Give me back that paper I signed, and go in peace."

Grim ignored the suggestion.

"Are you known to this sheikh who calls himself the Avenger?" he asked.

"*Wallahi!* Am I known to him? He took the title of Avenger on account of me, when he swore to spill my blood in the dust! In the war I let myself be captured by the British rather than fall into his hands, for in those days I was not yet ready to take the field against him.

"Am I known to him! *Bismillah!* It was my knife that made the scar across his cheek! Not only does he know and remember me, but every man of his who sees that scar remembers me!"

"Then the Avenger will think I am you?" suggested Grim.

"Aye, and torture you with crucifixion on a dung-heap among the flies, after you have been well beaten."

"And my men will be considered your men?" Grim went on.

"Surely, and tortured too."

Grim made another long pause, and Ali Higg smirked in the belief that he had found the weak place in Grim's courage. But he winced when Grim countered calmly.

"So whatever my men and I do will be credited to you?"

"Allah!"

"So that if I fail I shall have added to the wrath of the Avenger?"

"As a man who takes a little stone and adds it to a mountain!"

"You'd better help," said Grim.

"As God is my witness, I am afraid to go against Ben Saoud the Avenger," answered Ali Higg. "Besides, what can I do? You have sent away my men — some in this direction, some in that."

"It was you who sent them away," Grim retorted. "All I did was to postpone their return. Now I'll give you one last chance to use your men on a campaign. After this once, peace!"

"*Mashallah!* What shall I do with peace? How then shall I get new camels?"

"Breed them."

"How shall I get provisions?"

"Till the oases. Sow and reap."

"How shall I make my name feared?"

"Make it respected. Was not Solomon the wisest man? Did he make war? Rather he held the scales of justice evenly, and men looked up to him."

"But the prophet Mohammed came after Solomon, and was wiser. He made war."

"I tell you, Ali Higg," said Grim, "you've made the last raid you ever will with impunity. It's none of my business to ruin you. I'd sooner see you establish yourself as a strong chief — strong enough to keep the peace in these parts, and keeping it fairly. But as Allah is my witness, Ali Higg, if you don't mend your ways the British will come and end them for you. What is more, I'll take the field myself against you, and not quit until your bones are bleaching. You may call me friend or enemy, but choose now. Which is it to be?"

Ali Higg grew fidgety, and his eyes shifted again. I didn't see what Grim stood to score by extracting a promise of friendship from such an obvious rogue; but you never know what Grim is driving at until it suits him to make it clear.

"Wallahi! If I say I am your friend," the Lion of Petra answered presently, "what shall prevent you from going to Saoud the Avenger and saying you are his friend?"

"True! What shall prevent?" said Grim.

"And joining him against me? For all men love to take the stronger side."

Ali Higg called for his water-pipe, and a woman brought it already filled with tobacco. She lighted it for him, and he ordered her gruffly to get out. He was evidently feeling pleased with himself over that piece of subtle reasoning.

There was silence for several minutes, during which Grim produced a cigarette, and old Ali Baba, grandfather and captain of our gang of thieves, came to the mouth of the cave to make sure that all was well. He excused himself by asking leave to send four men to feed our camels, and thereafter sat down just around the corner of the wall, where he could listen.

"Do you realize," Grim asked at last, "that if I proposed to take sides against you I would simply take and kick you over this cliff now?"

"Allah! That is not how friends talk."

"Yet I haven't even disarmed you. Instead, my *hakim* here has lanced your boils and —"

"Aye! Leaving me too sore and weak to take the field against any one! I would bastinado such a *hakim* if he were mine."

He looked meaningly at me, but drew small satisfaction from it, for I laughed. I dare say my hand was a fraction heavy with the presentation razor that turned that trick. I can skin a dead lion rather neatly, but no college of surgeons ever gave me its parchment benediction.

"I don't wish you to take the field," said Grim.

"*Il hamdul illah!* [Thank God!] What then?"

"I want your men."

At that the Lion of Petra swore a blue streak sixty seconds long of brimstone Arab blasphemy. There is no such language as Arabic to swear in. Not even the Missouri mule has kicked back at such scurrilous expletives. Ali Baba thrust his old wrinkled face around the corner and grinned.

"So that is the idea! So that is the foreign scheme! What son of sixty dogs imagines he can lead my men?"

"They might find themselves pretty soon without a leader otherwise," suggested Grim.

Ali Higg ceased smoking. Rage and tobacco and helplessness didn't seem to make a palatable mixture. To judge by his wandering eyes, one second he seemed to be making up his mind to dash past us in a bolt for liberty, the next he contemplated suicide in a duel to the death with Grim.

His left hand groped for his rifle behind him, but could not quite reach it without betraying what he intended. Narayan Singh rattled the butt of his own rifle on the cave floor, and I laid mine pretty ostentatiously across my knees. There was no need for Grim to feel disturbed, and he obviously didn't.

In fact, I think Grim was having a good time. I'm no fisherman myself, lacking that kind of patience and getting more enjoyment from the sports that call for strenuous exertion, but I've often seen on the face of some fellow angling for a big one pretty much the expression that Grim wore then. His lips were set in a firm smile, and his eyes shone.

"You will ask me for my wives presently," said Ali Higg with biting sarcasm.

"No, not all of them," Grim answered. "Only one."

"By the beard of the Prophet and my feet, what next! I have divorced Ayisha — you may have the baggage. Much good may she do you!"

"I witnessed the divorce," Grim answered, "so I did not count her as your honor's wife."

"What then?"

Now the Lion's anger began to weaken into fear as he guessed the drift of Grim's intention. You can't help feeling sorry for a tyrant in a corner as one phase after another of his helplessness dawns on him.

Grim eased the torture at once. A man like Ali Higg suffers more from beaten pride than we non-tyrants do from toothache.

"Never fear," he said; "I will not take Jael from you. I will either bring or send her back to you safely afterward, but she must come."

Ali Higg looked incredulous, enraged, suspicious, treacherous in turn, but made no answer. Another answered for him. There was an inner cave all hung with fine Bokhara embroideries, opening into that in which we sat. Jael herself stepped from the interior gloom, stood still for a minute facing us all, and laughed.

"Enough, Ali; I will go with him!"

When we had first met her she was dressed in man's clothes; but now, all jeweled with turquoise and amber, she wore the Bedouin woman's regalia, and it suited her style of beauty. The paleness of her freckled face was relieved by the veil that partly framed it, and although she must have been deathly tired after the recent adventure she looked younger and not so hard-drawn. Jael was a perfect name for her — so perfect that you wondered whether it was really hers and not adopted; you could easily imagine her driving a tent-peg through the temples of a sleeping foe.

"Peace, woman!" growled Ali Higg.

"Peace, Ali? How can there be peace unless we let this Jimgrim have his way? Refuse him, and we must deal with Saoud the Avenger. Agree with him, and he may show us a way. If he fails, we shall be no worse off. I go with him."

"Peace, woman, I say! Be silent!"

"Very well. I will go in silence. It may be thus that we shall contrive peace. But I surely go with him!"

"Thou shalt not!"

"Ali, I say I go with him!"

CHAPTER II

"Once before she called herself his wife, on half the provocation."

THERE is a certain type of captious critic who annoys me horribly. He is usually a person who, by dint of vinegary unbelief in those solid underlying qualities of human character that decide most issues, has destroyed all his own power to make good the grand assertion in that favorite song of Grim's and mine —

I am the master of my fate, I am the captain of my soul!

Such a man will tell you that Grim hadn't done much yet. He will say — for I have heard him in a dozen places; on occasion he would be a merely jealous official superior of Grim's, but now and then, too, an after-dinner glutton by the fireside — that my friend's fortuitous resemblance to Ali Higg had got us safely into Petra, and the rest was sheer luck. The same man would doubtless consider it a piece of luck that the sun got up at dawn this morning and that the U.S. hasn't recently defaulted on its bonds. All right; but why not use the luck?

Grim had used his, and improved on it. Narayan Singh has certain qualities of romantic manhood that have made a soldier of him, along with an ineradicable fault that has preserved him from promotion and obscurity. It was Grim who put Narayan Singh to work. Grim picked him out of the routine business in Jerusalem.

I have independent means enough to labor free of charge if I see fit, and a pretty wide experience of emergencies that has made me in a sort of way reliable without dulling my appetite for adventure in the world's by-ways. It was Grim, not any Government, who studied me from every angle when I called on him in Jerusalem out of curiosity, put me to the test in a dozen ways without caring whether I suspected it or not, and bent my liking for adventure to his own ends. He did it with my permission, but not on my advice. And there wasn't another man in the Near East who could have made those seventeen thieves of ours risk their necks behind him without hope of loot.

You may say it was gall that let him make such dangerous use of other people, and I'll agree with you. Don't you admire a man with gall, provided it's not his own profit or some mere commercial end he's serving? I take it Drake had gall, and John Paul Jones, and Theodore Roosevelt as well as others whose memory more men cherish than the haters of the great prefer to think. I'm not one of those who choose to discredit any man who does things.

And it was luck and gall in combination, if you like, that now gave him the use of an "army" of a hundred and forty men, with a woman to captain them whose brains had been the making of Ali Higg. I won't say much for her military judgment, because we had captured her too easily for her to boast on that score; but she had the gift of bending Arabs to her will, and you know how it goes in politics — if you own the man who can swing the votes, the election is yours. The same principle applies in other walks of life.

I have heard a missionary criticaster say that because Ali Higg's army was mounted on stolen camels and fed on looted grain, as well as armed for the most part with rifles filched from the Allies, therefore Grim should have scorned to make use of it. But a quarter of a century ago I left off arguing with men like that. In the midst of un-westernized knavery Grim always uses the least unmoral weapon he can find, and makes the most of it.

We followed him out of the cave now to the narrow path that wound along the face of the cliff to a point where it met a flight of ancient steps something like a mile long. The ancients who carved Petra out of sandstone evidently didn't mind a toilsome climb to church, for there was a place of sacrifice at the top of the hill. We sat down beside Ali Baba in a row with his men, overlooking the Roman amplitheater, whose tiers and tiers of stone seats glittered in the sun.

The valley two hundred feet beneath us, inside the amphitheater and all about it, was black with goat-hair Bedouin tents, in which the wives and daughters of Ali Higg's army were busy with their morning work of doing nothing, leisurely. There were eagles soaring above us, whose shadows raced on the dazzling rock below, and innumerable kites were circling on about a level with our eyes. You could some-times catch the bronze sheen on their backs and watch the play of their wing-tips as they swerved. Along a ledge on the opposite cliff sat a row of vultures in fair imitation of us.

The colors of the Grand Canyon of the Colorado are about the same as those of Petra — the raw, real color out of which the paint for the universe was mixed, with the hard light from a polished turquoise sky to judge it all by, provided your brain will work in front of any such kaleidoscope. But we weren't there for the view.

"We'll give Jael Higg a chance to talk her old man round," said Grim in English; and Ali Baba caught the gist of it.

He knew enough English in the old days to rob tourists when the Turks weren't looking, and enough Turkish to cheat the police over the commission afterward.

"Whatever talking a woman does — and especially that woman — is the woof of trouble, Jimgrim," he said warningly.

But I saw other trouble coming, and laughed aloud, for which I cursed myself a moment afterward. A laugh is pretty easily misun-derstood in that land.

The cliff bulged outward on our left beyond the opening of Ali Higg's cave, and around the bend there was another cave that we hadn't investigated; but judging by the chatter of female voices it was the headquarters of Ali Higg's harem. He evidently overrode the rule about providing a separate establishment for each additional wife.

AROUND that corner now Ayisha came — Ayisha the divorced — with all her belongings done up in a huge blue bundle, and the whole lot balanced on her head. The wives of a polygamist are not, I believe, noted for lying down together like the leopard and the kid of prophecy, and a chorus of mocking laughter followed her.

Seeing and hearing me cough out that unconsidered "Aha!" she naturally supposed me to be mocking her too, and we were mortal enemies from that minute. At least, she was my mortal enemy, and I haven't learned yet how to keep an affair like that strictly one-sided.

I once knew a man who kept a female panther for a pet; he used to say the dear thing only needed humoring, but I remember attending his funeral, because there wasn't any parson and I had to read the service. I kept the panther's hide for a souvenir — with a neat round hole between the eyes to show how she and I made friends at last. You couldn't help thinking of a panther when you saw Ayisha angry.

Balancing the enormous bundle — full of the loot of villages, no doubt — with the grace that is born in the Bedouin women, she made as if to pass us, and I think she would have done so if Grim hadn't spoken, for she was proud.

"*Ya Sit Ayisha* [O Lady Ayisha], what have I done that you should treat me scornfully?" he asked.

"Have a care!" groaned Ali Baba.

Having raised sixteen sons and grandsons, he posed as an authority on women.

She turned to face Grim, her body quivering like a fine Damascus blade as she balanced the load. He smiled up at her, and she seemed to waver between liking for him and disgust at me. Then with the sudden swiftness of a female panther making up her mind, she answered his smile with melting eyes and flashing teeth, and opened the war with me by dumping the bundle into my lap.

It would have damaged a smaller man, for it weighed more than a hundredweight and there were brass bowls in it, and knives and things like that; but I caught it on knees and shins, and, although I didn't plan to, kicked it forward so that it rolled over the edge of the path and fell two hundred feet on to the ruined roof of an ancient tomb below.

You know how a panther lays his ears back? She expressed anger just as effectually, even if you couldn't say exactly how she did it. It wasn't any use apologizing. I sat rubbing my shins, with both eyes watching for the dagger I felt sure would come my way in a second. But she passed the buck to Grim.

"Kill that fool for me," she commanded him, and he laughed at me whimsically sidewise.

"But I need the man," he said. "He is the *hakim*. He has the chest of medicines. Who else shall physic us?"

"Bah!" she exclaimed. "I would bastinado such a fool. He is the son of sixty dogs who gave me baby's pap instead of poison for the Lion in there. Thanks to that fool I am divorced instead of a widow. Throw him down after my baggage!"

"We can recover most of it, and what has been broken shall be replaced," Grim answered. "What are your plans, O Lady Ayisha?"

"I go to find my people."

"Where are they?"

"Only Allah knows."

You see, the desert hasn't changed much. Hagar did the same thing once, going out alone into the waste of sand and rock, in search of a tiny wandering tribe whose tents are here today and gone tomorrow; and thousands since have done the same thing, without enough acquaintance with the angels to get water whenever they need it.

"Be seated," said Grim, and she took him at his word, thrusting herself down between him and me, giving me the point of her elbow.

I shifted along close to Ali Baba so as to allow her a full six feet of clearance, still bearing that possible dagger in mind.

"And now," growled Ali Baba in my ear, "the *bint* [girl, in a pejorative sense] believes she has him. He has bidden her sit beside him before witnesses, and has promised her a new outfit. Once before she called herself his wife, on half the provocation; and now who shall deny her?"

"He will," I answered. "Jimgrim is no Arab. We don't do things that way in the West."

"This is the East," he retorted, "and she will do things *her* way. *Inshallah* [If God wills], Jimgrim may prove clever enough to foil her, but I doubt it."

But more than cleverness was going to enter into Grim's dealings with that young woman. He was smiling, and a hint of worry underlay the smile. Nobody but a born fool would think of applying Western standards to judge her conduct by, and though she had meant to poison Ali Higg there wasn't a doubt she had lots of provocation. It was true we hadn't invited her to poison him; but she had made the attempt on Grim's account none the less, and we had taken full advantage of it.

If Grim had been disposed to leave her at a loose end I wouldn't have agreed to that; and even the wild Lothario, Narayan Singh, I think, would have objected. But Grim would be the last man to leave her unprovided for; I have seen him spend his scant spare hours befriending murderers whom he has landed in the jail.

"We go south to deal with Saoud, who calls himself the Avenger," Grim said to her. "Will you come with us?"

"I go where my lord wishes," she answered in the sort of voice that Ruth may have used to Boaz in the Bible story. Ruth came from that desert country too.

She must have known that Grim was an American, but I really think she meant what she said. Out in the sunlight there he was a lot better-looking than Ali Higg, because his face wasn't seamed by vice and anger; and she had grown so used to being owned by a man who resembled Grim superficially that it wouldn't be much of a task to transfer her affections. Grim for one thing had no other wife, and did not bastinado people.

"Until you find your people or another husband you must regard me as a father," Grim said kindly.

"But why should I look for another husband?" she asked.

That highly interesting question wasn't answered just then. Jael Higg came out, looked at the two of them, and laughed in that mean, metallic way that women use to one another. But I think that she, too, suspected that there might be a dagger to reckon with, for she made no direct comment.

"I am ready," she said in English. "My husband has agreed to my going with you. I shall bring a woman to keep me in countenance, but —" she glanced brazenly down the line of our men and raised her voice, finishing the speech in Arabic. " — I don't suppose there will be a man among you rash enough to try any liberties!"

I guess she was right, too, for her thin lips weren't of the yielding kind.

Some spirit of devilment took hold of me then; and, forgetting my rôle of Indian *hakim,* I horned in with a suggestion.

"Won't Ayisha serve the purpose, Lady Jael?"

Well, that woman was used to handling men by brow-beating and overbearing them. I suppose she had tongue-lashed into subjection some of the toughest characters between the Dead Sea and the Persian Gulf, and you get out of the habit of mincing words when that sort of job occurs frequently. You get fluent — acrid — fiery; or at least that had happened to her.

And she turned loose the full flood of her vocabulary on to me, speaking past Ayisha as if that young woman never existed, but making it perfectly obvious that we might divide the epithets between us. I dare say some of it was meant for Grim, too.

The fact was that the situation had got on her nerves, and all her pent-up rage had to find some sort of outlet. I had simply provided her an outlet; and Grim his opportunity.

He waited until she had finished, and then got to his feet and yawned.

"Let's have a clear understanding on two points to begin with, Lady Jael," he said in English. "I'll answer for my men. And two women on this expedition are enough."

The effect was as if he had struck her. She flinched away from him, and he followed up before she could recover and give tongue.

"I'll give all the orders. Everybody else obeys."

She bit her lip and turned her back on him. And then I realized that Ali Higg had been quietly watching us from inside the cave. She wasn't used to being rebuked in front of him. He came out and stood in the entrance, smiling ironically. I don't think he knew any English, but he appreciated that that termagant head wife of his had met a man who wasn't in the least afraid of her, and who knew how to manage her; and he looked almost good-tempered as he watched that happen that he had never been able to achieve.

"Call Yussuf," ordered Grim, producing his writing-pad and fountain pen, and sitting down again as if the incident were closed.

Now Yussuf was the spy, you may remember, with a home in Jaffa, who had brought word to Ali Higg about the plans and disposition of the British army in Palestine, and had fallen into our hands on his way back — a very dark-skinned man with little gold earrings, whose normal profession was spying for both sides to any quarrel. He was shoved along the ledge from his place at the end of the line by Ali Baba's men, and stood shifting from one foot to the other in front of Grim, clasping his hands first in front and then behind him as he watched Grim write.

Grim made considerable fuss with two envelopes, addressing both and sealing one inside the other. He evidently wanted to be seen doing that — wanted Ali Higg to see it; so I asked him in Arabic —

"Why two envelopes?"

There was no need to answer me, because Ali Higg made it clear that he was watching and listening. Jael, too, swallowed down her rage and faced about. Grim addressed himself to Yussuf.

"What do you want me to do with you?" he asked.

"Father of irony! What a question! Jaffa is my home. I was on my way thither when your honor decided otherwise. As a fish yearns for the sea I long for Jaffa."

"Can you make your way alone?"

"Inshallah."

"Would you like to try?"

"Give me but your permission and a camel, and see me put the telegraph to shame!"

"If I give you a letter to take to Jerusalem, will you deliver it?"

"Father of surprises! What is in the letter? Shall I carry then an order for my own arrest?"

"No. But there is an order inside that you are to be paid a full week's wages as a messenger, provided you deliver the letter without delay."

"Allah ykafik anni! [God reward you on my behalf!]"

"You know what will probably happen if Ali Higg's men catch you?"

"Trust me! I know the dogs! They will find it easier to catch the wind!"

"And you know what will happen to your Jaffa property if you try to play a trick on me?"

"Your honor had no need to say that. I am a loyal man."

"I know you for a spy-for-both-sides," answered Grim. "If one overtook you on the way and offered you money for the letter I shall give you, it would be your natural course to take the money and let the letter go. That is why I warn you about your Jaffa property. If you part with the one you shall lose the other."

"Trust me!"

"I don't trust you. I offer you payment and impose conditions. I give you clearly to understand that failure to deliver that letter in Jerusalem will involve a definite and heavy penalty. Now choose; will you carry the letter or remain here?"

"As well ask a thirsty man what he will do for a drink of water! Give me the letter!"

Grim gave it to him, and Jael returned into the cave to talk with Ali Higg. Despite the booing she had recently received, Ayisha got up and walked back toward the women's quarters as if she had forgotten something, and we saw no more of her for several minutes.

Grim's whole manner changed instantly. With a glance over his shoulder to make sure that neither Jael nor Ali Higg could see him, he pulled out a loaded Army revolver from under his cloak and passed it to Yussuf along with a handful of extra cartridges.

"Now go!" he ordered in a low voice. "One of Ali Baba's sons shall go below with you and pick you out a camel. Ride straight for that oasis where Ali Higg's army is camped."

"But they will capture me!"

"Listen, will you? If you go now you'll get there about nightfall. I don't think they'll be there, but if you see their camp-fires, make your camel kneel, and wait until they're gone. Better approach the oasis from the northward. They'll move off toward the south. The minute they're out of sight, feed your camel and then make for El-Maan; from there on to Jerusalem the way is easy."

"But —"

"You have your orders. Go!"

One of Ali Baba's sons went along with him to select a camel, and nobody except Yussuf worried on that score. We all knew which critter he would get; there was only one worthless specimen. Old Ali Baba laughed.

"The crows will say Allah is kind!" he remarked. "They would prefer to pick the bones of a fatter man, but any corpse is meat to them. Both Jael and the Lion know he carries that agreement. Father of ruses, he will be dead and they will have the letter before midnight; but why? What is to be gained by that?"

"Nothing," Grim answered. "But he'll live and they won't have it, if you ride hard."

"I?"

"Surely — you. The men at the oasis know you. I'm going to give you another presently, which Ali Higg will sign, ordering Ibrahim ben Ah to take those men southward at once and meet us at a place in the desert half-way between here and Abu Lissan. Take the best camel we've got, and keep to the southward. You'll reach the oasis well ahead of Yussuf.

"The Lion is sure to want to send either Jael herself or one of his own men instead of you; but I shall insist on your going. Then either the Lion or Jael will probably give you another letter with secret orders to Ibrahim ben Ah to capture Yussuf, kill him or bribe him, and take his letter from him.

"They'll very likely bribe you; in that case accept the bribe, but don't do what they say. Tear their letter up, or burn it in the desert. I think Yussuf will get through; at any rate, I've given him his chance."

"And if not?" I interrupted.

"Then, as Ali Baba remarked, the crows will eat him."

"That's Yussuf's end of it," said I. "But how about us? There'll be nothing then to keep the Lion and Jael from turning on us. They'll have that precious letter to the bank back, and —"

"Not they," Grim answered, smiling. "That letter to the bank is still in my pocket. If by some accident they happen to capture Yussuf all they'll find out is that I didn't give it to him after all. If they don't capture him — as I hope they won't — they'll still think he had it.

"They're likely not to turn on us until they've got that piece of paper back, but they'd surely try to murder me if they believed it was on my person. I'd sooner they had it in for Yussuf. And at that, we've given Yussuf a better chance for his life than he'd have had if we left him here with Ali Higg."

He said all that in English to me in a low voice, and Ali Baba, leaning past me to listen, picked only a word out here and there. I had to translate it for him; and when I had finished he sat meditating for a minute or two with an expression on his wrinkled old face like that of a man watching a motion picture — as if somewhere in the distance he were visualizing all the details on a screen.

"*Wallahi!* That is good," he said at last. "I am an old man. I lack sleep; and my bones are weary. But a man can play such a part proudly. There is cunning in it. Allah! What a thief was lost when Jimgrim took to soldiering!

"I will carry word for him to Ibrahim ben Ah if it is my last ride, and if they crucify me at the other end! But I am an old fox and, *inshallah,* no fool follower of Ali Higg shall suspect me of a trick."

He was so enamored of the plan that he had to get his sons and grandsons in a circle on the ledge and explain it all to them, pointing out the pros and cons of it, and delivering a final lecture on the general art of practicing deception.

"None of us would ever have been in jail if we had known as much as Jimgrim," I heard him say. "Observe: Jimgrim has their order on the bank for fifty thousand pounds. Let us suppose that Ali Higg and his wife Jael are the police. They know he has it. Does he bury it? Does he run away? He is no such fool. He lets them see him give it to another; he provides as far as possible that the other shall get safely away; and all the while he keeps the order in his pocket!

"Remains nothing but to provide a messenger for the police, who will surely not deliver their message; and he thinks of that too! Learn, ye dullards! Learn from Jimgrim, and there shall be no such thieves as ye in Asia!"

It ALL worked out exactly as Grim had foreseen. He wrote out a letter in Arabic to Ibrahim ben Ah in the oasis, ordering him to take those hundred and forty men of Ali Higg's to a point nearly due south, about half-way between Petra and Abu Lissan. Then he interrupted Ali Higg and Jael in the cave where they were whispering together, and requested the Lion to sign it. The Lion took his time, reading the letter two or three times over, and Jael offered to go down to the camp below and find a man who would carry it.

"I will send one of my men," answered Grim, and it seemed she had already learned better than to argue with him.

So while the Lion gained time by studying the letter and asking Grim a lot of random questions Jael went out and, taking care to turn her back to me, asked in a low voice who was the man who would carry a letter for Jimgrim.

Ali Baba stood up at once. She walked past him and signed to him to follow her just out of sight around the corner of the cliff. Whatever took place there must have agreed with Ali Baba's appetite, for he came back with his old eyes gleaming. He watched her return into the cave and then turned to his sons.

"I drove a good hard bargain with the daughter of corruption!" he remarked, and they all nodded.

I never found out how much she gave him, but dare wager that he extracted every sou the traffic would stand.

A minute after that Grim came out with the order for the "army" and sent the old man packing; after which Narayan Singh had a word to say. Grim always listens alertly when Narayan Singh speaks; for that long-headed Sikh would be fit to command an army if it weren't for one little peculiarity. About once in six months he is as likely as not to parade without his pants, and until the fumes of whisky die away the things he will say to his beloved colonel wouldn't get past any censor. He doesn't get punished much because he's such a splendid soldier; but they can't very well promote him.

"As I understand it, *sahib,* the purpose is to clip this Ali Higg's claws and yet save him from being wiped out by his enemies."

Grim nodded.

"He has two little armies. One, of a hundred and forty men under Ibrahim ben Ah, is to work with us?"

Grim nodded again.

"The other, of four and forty men, is up somewhere in the hills hereabouts?"

"Somewhere near the Beni Aroun village. They've been raiding it."

"And all the men that are left to Ali Higg are old ones and weaklings — sick, wounded and what not?"

"True. What of it?"

"This Ali Higg is a devil, Jimgrim *sahib*. He has a bad name. The enemies of such as he will be swift to take advantage. If you wish to see the last of him, good; leave him here with his handful."

"I have nine piasters in my pocket; that would be a too high price to pay for a lease on the Lion's life in that event. If you wish him to continue to hold Petra, better let him call in the other four-and-forty."

Grim laughed curtly.

"We'll not only let him have those men, Narayan Singh, but we'll provide him a good reason, too, for keeping them in Petra and not clapping them on our trail to pounce on us while we sleep."

"Shall we sleep here?"

"Not if I know it!" answered Grim.

Having nothing better to do, and rather liking to exercise my wits with puzzles, I watched the eagles and tried to figure out what Grim might do to keep the Lion of Petra and his four-and-forty occupied. I thought of a hundred and one obviously futile stunts, but not one that would have fooled me if I had been Ali Higg. I asked Narayan Singh what he would do in the circumstances.

"That will be a simple matter, *sahib*," he answered.

So I bawled him out suitably, not seeing why a Sikh should put on airs with me.

"Any ignorant fool can say a thing looks simple," said I. "You know no more than I do what the answer is."

"Seeing it is I most likely who must do the *bandobast*, that may be true," he answered patiently, "for many an ignorant man has served a purpose in his day. I will see now if our Jimgrim thinks as I do."

And instead of telling me his plan he went and talked with Grim in undertones. Grim nodded.

Meanwhile Ayisha had returned and was sitting quietly by, with her back to the wall of the cliff and an expression of masked alertness. They talk a lot about the fatalism of the East, and especially of its women, but in the sense in which the word is usually understood I have not seen much of it. I suppose you might call a cat watching a mouse-hole a fatalist.

Ayisha was watching points, and as alert for opportunity as ever was the brightest Broadway chorus lady. Given the right garments and a little training, she would have looked well in the front row of a chorus, by the way, for she had a splendid figure and could show her teeth.

Narayan Singh returned and sat down beside her. He looked amorous, the ability to do that being part of his equipment as a soldier. His great black beard was a little bit unkempt and his turban slightly awry, but liquid brown eyes and a flashing smile made up for all that.

"Father of bristles, what do you want?" she demanded; for he sat so close that she had to pay attention to him.

"Sweetheart," he answered, "you know I have loved you since the moment we first met."

"As a hog loves truffles," she retorted.

I thought that was a pretty poor beginning, but Narayan Singh is one of those soldiers who are only spurred to greater daring by defeat in the first few skirmishes.

"Nay, but as the bright sun loves a flower," he boomed. "Consider destiny, and wonder at it. Here was I born half a world away, hurled into wars and plucked forth with only a wound or two, sent on the wings of fortune into foreign lands and preserved by endless miracles from death and marriage, simply that I might meet thee, O lady with the eyes of a gazelle!"

Experts I have talked with say that all women should be carried by direct assault. I don't profess to know. But could you make love to a woman that way, with nearly twenty people looking on?

Our Arabs had started a game with dice, since the prospect of death had lost immediate interest; but they left off to watch and listen. Realizing that he had an attentive audience, Narayan Singh began to show his real paces.

He did not propose, though, to admit he was a Sikh in that land of Moslem fanatics. Our men all knew his true religion and nationality, but that was no reason why Ayisha should.

"We Pathans," he boasted, "understand the royal road of love! Our hearts burn within us and our spirits blaze when we at last meet the women of our destiny. And oh, what fortune for the woman who is loved by one of us! For we are men — strong, fiery-blooded men, whose arms are a comfort for our women and a terror to our foes. Hah! Lady Ayisha, smile and bless Allah, who has brought a Pathan of the Orakzai to lay his fortune at your feet!"

"Pig!" she answered.

Possibly she had overheard him say just now that his fortune amounted to nine piasters; that would be, say, forty-five cents at the old rate of exchange.

"Nay, lady, call me lover! Never was such burning love as mine! You doubt it? For a smile of yours I would pull the King of England off his throne and take the jewels of his crown to make a necklace for you.

"Behold: We march today against this braggart at Abu Lissan who calls himself the Avenger. A bold one, is he? A captain of eight hundred men? What do you covet of his? His ears? His nose? His head wife for a servant? Say the word and see! Test my love, beloved! Put it to the proof!"

His avowal was saved from entire absurdity by the fact that he had made the same sort of advances to her most of the way from Hebron; so she had a right to consider that he meant it, even if the proposal did not charm. She who had deliberately laid her net for Grim, in a land where all except the properly negotiated marriages are affairs of sudden fancy and violent abduction, could hardly doubt his earnestness. And, as I have said, all she was watching for was opportunity.

"You would not lift a hand for me," she answered. "Everybody knows the Pathan."

"Not lift a hand for thee, beloved! Hah! I would murder kings!"

"Nor would you tell me one secret."

"Try me! I would break open a king's letter, if thy tender eyes as much as glanced at it!"

"You would tell me anything?"

"Anything! By Allah and the devil's bones, I would tell you anything! We Pathans are no half-lovers!"

"Very well. Then tell me what to do to please Jimgrim," she answered.

He contrived to look thoroughly indignant. It was a good piece of acting. Jealousy blazed from his eyes.

"Do you want me to slay Jimgrim?" he demanded.

But she could act too. She smiled swiftly, as if his passionate avowal had not been quite without effect.

"Unless I please Jimgrim," she answered, "he might send me away; and then how could I listen to your boastings?"

"Ah!" he answered. "All lovely women have the wisdom of a snake! That is true. That is good reasoning. He might dismiss you. Ah! Well, listen then, beloved. Ali Higg has four-and-forty men, who will presently return to this place. It would please Jimgrim to know for a certainty that they will remain here, and not follow to attack us from the rear.

"Therefore go thou, beloved, and say to the wives of those men in the camp below there that our Jimgrim has promised two of them apiece to us, his men. Say that our going is but a ruse; that we shall return when the four-and-forty have left Petra and carry off our pick of the women.

"You may as well add that the only way to prevent that will be for them to keep their husbands close at hand. Thus you will satisfy Jimgrim."

She turned that over in her mind for half a minute and then got up without answering him. She did not even glance at any of us, but walked straight away along the narrow ledge, and started down the ancient stone stairway toward the women's camp.

As soon as she was out of earshot Narayan Singh looked over toward me and showed his white teeth in a perfectly prodigious smile.

"That is the way in which such things are done, *bahadur!*" he remarked.

CHAPTER III

"We're all set now."

THOSE four-and-forty men of Ali Higg's who had been raiding the Beni Aroun village were a much too dangerous factor for Grim to take unnecessary chances with. Ali Higg, Jael and Ayisha were accounted for; we knew nearly every detail of their movements since we entered Petra. But there were other women, whom we had hardly more than seen, and some whom we had not seen; to say nothing of the handful of men described by Narayan Singh as the "weak and wounded," whose number we did not know exactly, and one of whom might have left in secret to bring the four-and-forty in.

It was likely we could fight the four-and-forty and escape without more than a fair proportion of casualties. But with only twenty men all told we couldn't afford to lose one; and there were the Bedouin women in the camp to be reckoned with. They are pretty fierce, those women. Lawrence held Petra with a scratch regiment of them in one of his most famous battles, and thoroughly routed Turkish regulars, who are not troops to be despised. And now that Ayisha was spreading among them the report of our intention to carry off the youngest and best-looking there was more than a chance that they night send a messenger on their own account to summon their husbands in a hurry.

That trick of Narayan Singh's was one of those boomerang contrivances, in other words, that have to be snappily handled. If we were out of the way before the husbands returned, well and good; they were extremely likely to insist on staying in Petra to defend their women; but if they should return before we were out of the way, they would almost certainly attack us as the best means of preventing what we were supposed to contemplate.

So although we all needed sleep, and although Ali Higg importuned Grim to spend that night in Petra — doubtless for private reasons not unconnected with those four-and-forty men, although he made a great to-do about hospitality — Grim wasted no more time. And there was another reason. The women were not wholly without true ground for anxiety.

Our Arabs were professionals from El-Kalil, the home of the proudest trained thieves in the world. Thieving, to them, made the combined appeal of sport and guild craftsmanship; and there seems to be no such exhilarating sport as stealing women, that being the one game in the world that knows no national boundaries. Now that Ali Baba was away, whose word was absolute law to his sons and grandsons, the sixteen were not going to be any too easy to control — not with a bait like that Bedouin camp under their acquisitive noses.

When Grim announced himself ready to start, there were only

eight of them in sight. The rest had vanished, and there was only one direction they could have taken — down that mile-long flight of stone steps. Thereafter there were two ways — to the left toward "Pharaoh's Treasury" where our camels waited; to the right in the direction of the women's tents. It was a safe bet which way they had gone.

Most people think that generalship consists solely in the art of winning or losing battles, but there couldn't be a greater mistake. If that were really so, then chessplayers would conquer the world, and all our armchair theorists would be enthroned as an aristocracy.

It is soldiers who win battles. The good general is the man who can get them to the spot without leaving more than a third of them behind in clink and another third in hospital. The hardest test of a man's manhood lies in leadership. Can he or can't he make the lame dog and the rascal so respect him that they'll disregard their own immediate comfort and profit, and give their best behind him in the cause he favors?

Of course, no two men are quite alike in their methods, and there aren't any definite rules, or we'd all learn them and all want to lead. Ali Higg's methods, for instance, were crucifixion or the bastinado for disobedience; Jael's was something like it, with scarifying language for milder cases. She looked at our diminished line, and glanced at Grim, and smiled ironically.

"Let's go," said Grim.

So off we marched along the overhanging ledge, Grim leading, Jael next, then Narayan Singh, then I, followed by our remnant bringing up the rear, chorusing abuse of Ali Higg for a mean host who had given them no presents. The Lion of Petra stood in the cave-mouth watching us with an expression such as you can see in New York any day on the face of an obvious criminal who has been acquitted on a technicality — near-incredulity, relief, cunning, and contempt for authority that can't convict him.

It seemed to me merely a question of how many hours it would take that tough Lion of Petra to recover from the lancing of his boils before he would set out to avenge himself on our rear. Men of his ambitious mold think more, as a rule, of personal vengeance than of high strategy; they are made short-sighted by the very qualities that have brought a semblance of success.

Without Jael to counsel him he wasn't likely to betray much wisdom, and we had her in control; but she and Ali Higg had done a lot of whispering together in the cave, and although I'm no kind of judge of women, not having had much opportunity to learn the home-keeping sciences, I was ready to bet that minute that a plan was in the wind for cooking our goose thoroughly.

And so, as it transpired, there was; but not even Grim, who can see farther than most men through the fog of any Eastern entanglement, had the remotest suspicion of what its form was going to take.

If it had been my business I would have turned to the right at the foot of that ancient stairway. Having handled lawless natives by the score in various parts of Africa, my method would have been to go into that women's camp and rout my rascals out of it with a heavy fist for those I could overtake and a long whip for the rest of them. Grim turned straight to the left and never said a word, merely nodding recognition of Ayisha as she came along and joined us.

When we passed the mass of ruins on to which I had dropped Ayisha's bundle of belongings he sent two men to climb and fetch it. The force of the fall had burst it open, but Ayisha had enough faith in the future to stand by and make sure that they filched nothing, so, though the things were all scattered about and a few bits of hardware were smashed, the total loss didn't amount to much. I thought it a good chance to try to make friends again, and offered to pay her cash for the damage.

"Better laugh at me now while you dare," she retorted. *"Inshallah,* when the time comes you shall pay with all you have!"

I was sorry for her, and didn't feel like laughing, yet what else was there to do? If I had appeared to take her threat seriously that would only have flattered her malicious instinct and made matters that much worse.

Glancing upward at the ledge, I could see the Lion of Petra standing watching us, also contemplating mischief. She had been taught in his school and, like him, would certainly take a yard for every inch you yielded. So I did laugh — and regretted it later.

"You scare me out of my poor wits," said I.

"Since when has an Indian had wits?" she answered. "Allah made Indians to be the scorn of all decent folk!"

Wouldn't you have felt flattered by that? I did. If I had come so far without betraying my nationality to that young woman's keen perception it was likely I might go the rest of the way without failing Grim. And isn't it remarkable how an unexpected discovery like that sets you to exaggerating all the by-play with which you have hitherto half-unconsciously contrived a deception? All the way to Pharaoh's Treasury I walked, scratched myself, spat, belched and volunteered comments like an Indian, until Narayan Singh laughed at me.

"Has the *sahib* heard the fable of the man who would be king?" he asked. "No? He acted so like a king in advance that the people decided he would be no novelty, and did away with him."

There was something in what he said. If you act a part instead of thinking and being it, they'll find you out. So I left off playing Indian.

I told in the last story all about that fabled Treasure House of Pharaoh — really a temple to Isis, that stands facing the twelve-foot gap in a cliff, which is Petra's only entrance gate. Our camels knelt where we had left them in the shade of the enormous porch, and grumbled at being loaded nearly as abominably as our eight Arabs did at having to do the work short-handed. They wanted to wait for the others, but Grim would have none of that; so they fired a last fusillade of shots at the great stone urn above the porch that every Bedouin believes to contain Pharaoh's jewels, and we started.

W E HAD crossed the intervening space, and Grim on the leading camel was already through the gap into the Valley of Moses, when I saw our laggards coming. They had additional camels with them, which we needed, having lost three in the skirmish when we captured Jael; but they had brought six, and three of the beasts were loaded. I called out to Grim, but he did not stop.

"Aha!" laughed Narayan Singh. "We shall now see what the major *sahib* has to say to stragglers!"

We were half a mile into the valley, at that point a quarter of a mile wide with six-hundred-foot cliffs on either hand, when they overtook us and formed the tail of our line. They said nothing, and none of the eight who had stayed with us made any comment. Part of the game was evidently to hope that Grim would take no notice, and as for the loot, that was all in the family anyhow. But hope that springs eternal isn't always blessed. Grim called a halt at last.

The fellow who had led the filching expedition was Mujrim, Ali Baba's oldest son, a man bigger than I am and about as heavy — a serene-browed, black-bearded, sunny-tempered fellow (when not crossed) and the logical captain of the gang in the old man's absence. Grim counted heads, found all present, and asked what the disappearance had meant. Mujrim spoke up for his brothers.

"We thought there were camels needed, so we went and procured them."

"Good," Grim answered. "Did you pay for them?"

"*Wallahi!* Who would pay thieves for something they had stolen?"

"What else did you bring?"

"Oh, a present or two. The Lion of Petra proved himself a mean man, for he gave us nothing except a meager bellyful up there on the ledge. But the women in the camp were ashamed of his meanness and treated us handsomely."

"Are the presents all in those bundles on the three camels?"

"Surely. Where else?"

"Nothing under your shirt, for instance?"

"Nothing."

"Let me see."

"By the bones of God's Prophet, Jimgrim, everything is in those bundles."

"If you're telling the truth, prove it. Let me see."

Neither smiling nor frowning, in fact giving no hint of his ultimate intention, Grim drove his camel closer; and Mujrim edged away, beginning to look worried, until at last he was alongside me and ready to go on retreating if Grim insisted.

"Search him, please!" said Grim.

I believe in obeying orders. You don't have to follow a man if you don't care for his leadership. I have chosen to differ from more than one man after the event, but never yet spoiled a leader's game by hesitating in a climax. Moreover, on one occasion when the leading was up to me I remember I beat a man half out of his senses for arguing with me in a pinch; whereas if he had chosen the proper time to air his views we might have agreed, or else parted good friends. And what is sauce for the goose is sauce for the gander. I laid my left hand on Mujrim's arm and thrust my right into the bosom of his shirt, bringing out a couple of amber necklaces worth at least a hundred dollars each.

I liked Mujrim from the first. I liked him even better in that minute. Ninety-nine Arabs out of any hundred would have pulled a knife at me. He struck me with his fist — a clean, manly blow above the belt, heavy enough to have knocked me out of the saddle if I hadn't expected something of the sort.

His brothers naturally drew their weapons. They probably expected me to draw mine. But I was satisfied for the moment to keep hold of the necklaces and be on guard against a second blow.

"Why strike the *hakim?*" Grim asked him. "He obeyed my order. His act was mine."

"*Mashallah!*" he retorted. "That is a wonder of a saying. If it is true, then it was you I struck. Behold, I strike again."

And he let out another blow at me that would have broken the arm of a weaker man.

"Patience, *sahib,* patience!" Narayan Singh whispered, edging his camel close to mine; but big-game hunting is a pretty good teacher of that.

It was clear enough that Grim was up against mutiny. Jael Higg was smiling jubilantly in that handsome, thin-lipped way of hers, and Ayisha was calling out aloud to Mujrim to "kill the cursed Indian and be done with it."

I kept my eye on Grim. He approached within arm's length, and for a minute I thought he was going to be crazy enough to accept the blows as having landed on himself, and strike back. In that event, unless Grim should use his pistol he was as good as dead, for the Arab's blood was up. But he chose to ignore the talk.

"We'll keep the camels and pay Lady Jael for them," he said quietly. "You and the other seven walk back and deposit what you call the presents in the Treasury, where the women will find them sooner or later."

"*Wallahi!* Am I dreaming? Who orders me to walk back?"

"Right smartly too!" Grim answered. "I'm not going to wait a week for you."

"Allah!"

Mujrim's face was black with rage by that time — the swift, volcanic temper of a lawless fellow checked. But even with the blood up back of his eyes I think he recognized that Grim meant to master him at all costs. There wasn't a trace of anxiety on Grim's face — nothing whatever but determination.

"I told you all clearly before we started that I'd have no looting on this trip," said Grim. "You can't take advantage of me just because Ali Baba isn't here. Carry that stuff back. I shall wait here and search you all when you return, so you'd better bear that in mind."

Remember, those weren't men who had had military training. Probably the only people they had ever obeyed were Ali Baba, whose lightest word was law, the jailer at El-Kalil during periods of imprisonment, and Grim himself. Mujrim was like a big dog with a bone in his teeth, and the pack gathered closer around him, ready to help him keep it.

"By the Prophet's feet," roared Mujrim, "these camels are all ours. We will find our father Ali Baba and return to El-Kalil. We are free men!"

"Free to obey me," Grim answered. "You weren't conscripted; you volunteered. Now, no nonsense! Get busy!"

It was touch and go for about ten seconds. I think if Grim had made a false move then, such as reaching for a weapon or using an oath, they would have carried out that threat and deserted us. The near-impossibility of finding Ali Baba, and the probability of all being killed by Ali Higg's men if they did find him, wouldn't have prevented them. But Grim made no false move.

I've always envied that ability in other men, rare as it is, to be utterly calm in the face of anger. I can use patience, as I've said, but that is a different thing altogether. Patience only exasperates, as often as not. I can keep my own hot temper in subjection; but it's there, and the other fellow usually knows that, with the result that I have had to fight in circumstances that Grim would have negotiated diplomatically. You can't be angry and convincing. I know that, for I've tried and failed too often.

Grim wasn't angry. Mujrim and the whole gang knew it. He had simply made up his mind that he was in the right and that it was a proper time to stand by what he knew; and it dawned on that gang of thieves that they would have to kill him if they proposed to have their own way.

I was close enough to Mujrim to read the changing emotions. He opened his clenched teeth a fraction, as most men do when they suddenly see the strength of an opponent's case. Then his sunny good nature came to the rescue. He opened his mouth wider — hesitated — spoke — and I knew that Grim had won.

"But it is too much to ask a man to walk back, Jimgrim!"

They were a first-class gang. I'm not discussing their profession, which was their affair, risks included. What I mean is that in a world in which most of us need no accuser, having consciences that truthfully blame ourselves, they had lots of redeeming manhood and less yellow in their makeup than afflicts some folk who never do anything wrong because they'd be afraid to. They loved that huge brother of theirs and were loyal to him.

They recognized instantly that he had yielded, and instinctively — swiftly — without any process of reasoning — they set to work to save his face and let him down lightly.

You never heard a more sudden chorus of abuse than they aimed at me. They knew I was an American, of course, but they were much too loyal to the practice of deception to rake that up, even in such a crisis. I was disguised as an Indian, and that was enough. They damned me as an Indian.

"The *hakim* struck him!"

"The cursed dog of a *hakim* thrust a hand into his bosom!"

"By what right does a *hakim* interfere with Mujrim?"

"Beat him!"

"It was the *hakim's fault! He insulted our brother! Who wouldn't have struck back?*"

"Is the *hakim* a coward?"

"Ha-ha! Does the *hakim* take a blow like an ass lying down?"

"The *hakim* is a coward! He insulted Mujrim and was struck for it, but daren't hit back!"

"Let the *hakim* pick our weakest man and fight him!"

"Good! True! It was the *hakim's* fault! Make the *hakim* fight! Give him his choice; Mujrim is too strong for him!"

Well, I suppose that ever since the world was concentrated out of chaos and old night whoever faced defeat has claimed a scapegoat. All I was interested in was lending Grim the full force of whatever attributes I have. I caught his eye, and he smiled whimsically, with one eyebrow curved into an interrogation mark.

The gang became silent suddenly — wondering whether I would dare accept the challenge; but I kept silent, too, for it was up to Grim. I knew he didn't doubt my willingness to fight; and I knew he would be the last man to refuse to make the fullest use of me; it was a question of diplomacy, which, as I have said before, is hardly my long suit.

"The *hakim* obeyed my order," he said at last. "Mujrim struck him. Mujrim therefore gave the insult. Let the *hakim* name what satisfaction he requires."

I didn't waste a second after that. It is one of my chief failings that I simply love a fight on equal terms. Men choose to differ about the name of the Power who parceled out men's attributes, but this one thing I know: I received my share of strength, and a most berserkerish delight in using it. "Are you afraid to fight me without weapons?" I asked, laughing into Mujrim's face.

His answer was to vault from his camel without a word, throw all his weapons on the ground, and start to strip himself. I followed suit, and the rest all *naak*-ed the camels in a wide semi-circle.

"Don't use your fists on him," Grim whispered. " 'Twouldn't be fair. These Arabs don't understand that gentle art."

Then he went and squatted on top of a rock facing the semicircle, to watch proceedings.

THE other men all squatted in front of the kneeling camels. Jael went and sat near Grim. Ayisha took up a position of her own on Grim's left hand, midway between him and the semicircle; and I had time to notice that both she and Jael were as eager for the spectacle as any one. After that I sized up my antagonist, and liked the look of him — as Narayan Singh, catching the clothes I tossed to him, did not.

"Stick a thumb in his eye if he strangles you, *sahib!*" he whispered.

Standards of ethics vary slightly as you travel farther East.

All either of us kept on were our cotton trousers, and there wasn't much to choose between us as the sun beat down on muscles bulging under healthy skin. I am a sunburned man, but my skin looked white and satiny against his coppery bronze. He had several inches the advantage over me in height and length of arm, and was pretty obviously quicker on his feet; but twenty years of roughing it have taught me not to trouble much about the other fellow's odds. The main thing is to reckon up your own, and discover his point of weakness.

"Are you both ready?" Grim called out, and we walked in and faced each other.

"Go!" he shouted, and Mujrim began to stalk me crab-wise with both arms thrust forward, looking for an opening.

One weak point became obvious at once. He considered himself a wrestler, and fully expected to rush me and win in sixty seconds. So I gave him the chance he looked for, and that first fall was easy; he went over my head on to his back on the sand with a thump that shook the wind out of him.

But all I scored by that, of course, was to spoil a little of his confidence. He wasn't likely to repeat such a mistake. He got to his feet pretty quickly, and I have seen a wounded lion look less pugnacious. The gang shouted a lot of good advice to him to wring my neck, kneel on my stomach, pull my arms out by the roots, and, in fact, to go in and rid the earth of me; and he threw one swift glance in their direction as much as to say he wouldn't fail them. Then I took the fight to him, and we closed.

Well, I've had many a good fight in my day, having to admit, with less shame than some think seemly, that I'm kind of willing to mix it with any strong antagonist who wants to take my number down. But, looking back, I think that was the best of all. It was rather spoiled at one stage by Mujrim's biting when I had him in a painful hold he could not break. But you can't expect a half-savage to act like a white man all the way, and he only tore an inch or two of skin loose. Besides, he made up for it handsomely before the end.

The game was fast, for one thing, which suits my temperament.

Middle age hasn't made me a dawdler yet. And as we rolled and tossed over and over, grunting, and sweating so in the sun that we could usually slip out of a hold as easily as break it, the speed took the gang by the heartstrings, and from time to time I had visions of Grim beating them off with his camel-stick as they crowded in to scream advice to their champion.

I never fought over so much ground before or since. I knew I had my man beaten, and Mujrim, I think, guessed it after the first five minutes; he seemed to think his only chance was to spread the battle over half an acre, dragging and rolling me this and that way with the idea of wearing me out. But I was the stronger of the two, and it was I who did the wearing down.

There came a moment when he lay under me and gasped, and I even had time to grow conscious of surroundings — a thing you can't do if the man you're up against is still fit to make you use all you've got. Then, in between the bass booming of Narayan Singh, I distinguished Ayisha's shrill voice screaming to Mujrim to tear my tongue out.

There is something barbaric in a woman's scream that puts new fight into most uncivilized folk, and especially into all the desert people. Mujrim must have heard that shrilling, for he suddenly revived, and over and over we went with nearly bursting muscles in a series of sudden spurts, until we lay panting again pretty close to Ayisha's feet. I couldn't see her, naturally, for my back was uppermost; and Mujrim had murder in his eye; I did not dare relax the pressure on him for a second. His right hand was groping wildly for a handful of my thigh muscles, and what she did was to slip a dagger into it.

His fingers closed on the thing before he realized what it was, and before Grim or any one could intervene. I didn't know what had happened. My eyes were full of sweat and dust in any case, and the trick took place behind me. But Mujrim, suddenly aware of what was in his hand, threw the thing away like the sportsman he was at heart; and the effort gave me my opportunity.

I got a sudden hold that pinned his left arm to his side — rose to my feet, lifting him with the old bag-heaver's hoist that uses every muscle in your body, and was considering whether the time had come to lay him pretty gently on his back, or whether he needed another shake-up, when something stung the calf of my leg as if a snake had bitten it.

At that there was an angry yell from everybody. I hurled my man clear of me, and Grim stepped in between us, stopping the fight. When I could get the sweat out of my eyes I saw there was blood running pretty freely down from my calf into my shoe. Grim stooped and picked up Ayisha's dagger. The minx had been so bent on seeing me murdered that when Mujrim refused to use the thing she had picked it up again and thrown it — fortunately doing no more harm than to open a cut two inches long that bled more freely than it hurt.

Mujrim was more annoyed than any one. He had all the exercise he needed, and lay on his back with his brothers all about him sluicing him with water from one of the camel-bags. He sent them to sluice me too, and called out to me between gasps for breath to be good enough to believe that the wound was none of his doing.

Ayisha was perfectly unconcerned about it. Beyond demanding the dagger back from Grim she made no comment. He gave it to her with the remark that if she should play a trick like that again he would have her hanged to the nearest tree; but she didn't believe him any more than I did, and showed her teeth in as merry a smile as ever lone bachelor set eyes on.

Jael, on the other hand, was indignant — not at my being wounded, for she wasn't exactly a stickler for ethics, and my welfare was no concern of hers — but because Grim should neglect such an obvious chance.

"The least you might do is to have the hussy beaten," she insisted. "You'll never make a leader of men, my friend. You don't know enough to be drastic. You're weak!"

Yet, if you ask me, I think Grim came out of it pretty well. There wasn't another word from the defaulters. Mujrim had been wrenched and bruised too badly to be fit for much for an hour or two, and it was out of the question to make him walk back. But Grim tossed the amber necklaces to one of the others, pointed with his stick toward the three camel-loads of miscellaneous "presents," and said his final say on that subject.

"Back you go now! Take those loads and walk!"

They went off without a murmur. And bear in mind that if there is one thing on earth that Arabs of their stamp consider beneath their dignity, it is to carry loads. They expect their women-folk to do that when camels or asses are not available.

Mujrim got to his feet after they had gone, and apologized to Grim handsomely.

"*Wallahi,* Jimgrim, you were in the right! There should be but one captain — and his word law, even when he says that white is black!"

It was pretty safe to say that looting was at an end as far as that expedition was concerned. And if you think, as I have heard some say, that it wasn't Grim, but I who pulled off that affair, I don't agree with you. You might just as well say that the cards had won a game, rather than the player of the hand; or that Bill Adams won the battle of Waterloo by killing eighteen Frenchmen with his saber. Hats off to Bill Adams, certainly; but the old Iron Duke was the boy who led trumps when the right time came.

I hate this modern craze for taking credit from every leader. Believe me, it takes a good man to persuade me to risk hair and hide in his behalf, as one or two of Grim's jealous critics might discover if they had the guts to try.

We sat down all together in the shadow of a great rock, women included, and discussed the fight from start to finish, each of the brothers claiming to know a hold that would have beaten me — which might easily be true, for I am no Gotch or Hackenschmidt — yet all equally averse to testing it. And presently Narayan Singh cut loose and told us wonderful lies about the wrestlers of Bihar and feats he had seen them perform at the marriage feasts of Indian rajas. A first-class romancer is my friend Narayan Singh, as well as a good soldier.

The rift in our lute was mended, not a doubt of it. That party under the rock in the Valley of Moses, where we drank warm water out of goatskin bags, smoked powdery imported cigarettes and bayed about our reminiscences like dogs over a kill, is one of the pleasantest I can remember.

It was nearly high noon, and the sun beat down the floor of the gorge between ragged cliffs, making the air suffocating. Every once in a while a gust of hot wind would pick up a cloud of dust and take it waltzing along the valley, spreading a gritty mixture of air and dirt that you could hardly breathe. One or two eagles soared sleepily against the turquoise sky, but the kites appeared to have had enough of the heat and were hiding somewhere.

Only the centipedes and scorpions beside ourselves seemed satisfied with conditions as they were; and they were about the only trouble we had. Narayan Singh said that it was the blood from the scratch in my leg that attracted them and it may be that he knew; but, as I have remarked before, he doesn't need much fact to weave a tale from.

The part I liked best was Grim's whole attitude. He might easily have spoiled the fun by doing what so many asses do — smothering with flubdub whoever happens to have done his bit. He knew exactly how useful in a pinch my strength and willingness to fight had been, and in case I didn't know it, too, he made one comment, and let it go at that:

"If Mujrim had beaten you we'd have had to call this expedition off. There'd have been no holding them. But we're all set now."

All the same, I thought that an exaggeration, unless he excluded Ayisha from the reckoning. The gang now referred to her constantly in her presence as "the woman Ayisha;" whereas before her swift divorce from Ali Higg in Petra she had always been "the Lady Ayisha" and "Princess." If she was "set" on any purpose, then it was on snatching her own chestnuts from the fire of fate; and whoever should seek to prevent her was going to suffer unless he watched his step.

I would have excluded Jael Higg, too, from the "all set" reckoning. She was devoting herself, rather cautiously just then, in that thin-lipped way of her, to being a good fellow, joining in the conversation and laughing readily in a rather pleasant voice, with no more than a symptom of underlying harshness. But her eyes were hard — iron-hard; and they glittered whenever she looked at Grim.

I think she regarded me, along with the Arabs and Narayan Singh, as a man whom she could find a way of managing in her own good time. But she was about as empty of forgiveness as a Red Sea shark.

In my judgment nothing less than Grim's utter ruin would ever satisfy her for capture and defeat at his hands, although she undoubtedly proposed to make the utmost use of his brains and altruism until her time should come.

They made a wonderful contrast, those two, sitting side by side under the rock — she with her freckled, smooth face and reddish hair showing under a black shawl; he with that ready smile, the puzzling, almost book-worm eyes, and the expression, even with his face framed in an Arab headdress, of a forceful, imaginative business man.

"You are a fool, James Grim," I heard her say to him. "You don't know which side your bread is buttered on. If you would cross the Jordan for good and all I could make you king of all this country in a year!"

"That, or vulture-food?" he asked her; and laughed, and lit a cigarette.

CHAPTER IV

"A cent for your sympathy."

WELL, our ruffians turned up at last, and brought back news with them. Ali Higg, they said, was on the rampage. He had left his aerie of a cave, and was superintending the saddling of a score of camels in front of "Pharaoh's Treasury."

"But not good camels, Jimgrim — mangy, miserable beasts. His men are using all the best ones, and those six splendid ones that we borrowed just now are all that were left of his private string. If he means to follow he will have hard work. He has collected a handful of men, but they are hardly better than the camels — fit food for kites — sick men, wounded men, men afraid of their own shadows — scarcely able to lift a camel-pack between them.

"We walked up to the Treasury and flung the plunder down, saying that our Sheikh Jimgrim declined to burden camels with such miserable stuff. He ordered his party of crows' meat to open fire on us; but one of them swore that our return with that loot must be a trick to start trouble. He said that you and the rest of our party were doubtless waiting close at hand to make reprisals, and the sound of the first shot would certainly bring you hurrying. The others, being all afraid, agreed with the first man.

"So we behaved like men who have been found out in a trick, carrying on scornfully and saying it was a pity nobody in Petra was brave enough to fight, since our Sheikh Jimgrim took no pleasure in defeating cowards. And what with one hot word and another we made our escape safely."

But that talk might have been a trick to cover up another one, and Grim made sure.

"Men who speak truth," he laughed, "are never afraid to prove it. Let's see how much loot you've still got hidden in your clothes."

They submitted to be searched with entire good humor, and Grim displayed an intricate knowledge of their ways of hiding things that made them laugh. But he had had his way; there wasn't as much as a woman's earring or a brooch among them, and they were all the better tempered for having proved it, considering now that the joke was as much on him as on themselves.

That is a great point, by the way, which some men fail to understand. When disobedience doesn't really matter much you can now and then afford to overlook it — especially if it would be easy to enforce discipline; because discipline that is easy to enforce doesn't make a lasting impression on naturally lawless men.

But in a tight place, when men disobey because they think they have you at a disadvantage, and to force the issue looks like sure disaster, then you can't afford to yield one jot or tittle of authority.

Better die there with your boots on than give way; because if you fail then you'll never regain their respect.

And having won your point, by hook or crook, brute force, profanity or argument, be sure you have the whole of it. To use Narayan Singh's expression —

"Milk the udders of obedience dry."

Thereafter whenever you concede a point or two you'll find it safe enough, because they will realize it is concession, and not anarchy.

We were all in a rare good temper now, Jael Higg not least of us. I suppose the news that Ali Higg was on the move was what raised her spirits. Grim asked her what she supposed the Lion intended, but she shook her head and laughed.

"You're worse than a divorce court! You separate a man and wife, and ask the wife to account for her husband's doings?"

"I know nothing of lions," Narayan Singh commented. "Mine is a land of tigers. When a tiger keeps quiet he is difficult and dangerous to trap. When he prowls he is easy."

At that Mahommed piped up, Ali Baba's youngest son, poet to the gang, and bard, and arch-inventor of impracticable plans.

"I say let us lie in ambush in this hot *jahannum* of a valley, and catch the Lion as he ventures out. Let us take him back with us to El-Kalil and lodge him in the jail for folk to make songs about."

The notion was not impossible on the face of it. There were plenty of suitable places for ambush, as Alexander of Macedon found out, for instance, when he tried to force that gorge. But it would only have entailed the breaking of Grim's promise and the absolute reversal of his stubborn principle, that he had no right to impose, and therefore would not move a finger toward imposing, alien rule on Arabia, even in the interest of peace, and indirectly. It was Grim's notion of duty and enjoyment — and a good one, too, in my opinion — to prevent that very thing by drawing the teeth of contention and giving the Arabs a chance to work out their own destiny.

"Let's go," he said; and the only members of the party to grumble at that suggestion were the camels, who object to everything.

When you bear in mind that none of us — not even the women — had slept a wink the previous night, and that we had to face the hot south wind that withers the Arabian desert, and, impinging on the northern wall of that gruesome Valley of Moses, blows like a furnace blast down the ever narrowing funnel, our high spirits were a thing to wonder at.

None of us had more than a vague idea of the danger into which Grim was leading us. My only objection to him is that exasperating way he has of never discussing difficulties until after he has thought out their solution.

In my own way I'm rather a cautious man. I like adventure, but I also like to puzzle out the chances in advance, both of risk and profit, and so be prepared for them. Having anticipated ten per cent or so of the possibilities, I can then devote more attention to the unexpected when it happens.

But the very method that annoyed me was like meat and drink to our rogues of followers. What they did not know didn't trouble them overmuch. Weaned on knavery, and used to haphazard devilment of any kind at all, all they asked of life was meat and drink, a chance to get away with other men's belongings, and something new as often as might be, to make up songs about.

To them Grim's very reticence was all in his favor, since it suggested mystery. And remember, that is the land where the tales now known in the West as the Arabian Nights first stirred men's imagination. They wouldn't have enjoyed things half as much if they had known exactly what was going to happen next.

Nor were they the only ones who enjoyed Grim's method. There was Narayan Singh. He rode his camel beside mine, and occasionally leaned across to boom remarks through the cloth that covered nose and mouth with the un-accomplishable purpose of defeating the hot wind.

"Hah! *Sahib,* this suits me! This is the true way of a soldier! Here today and gone tomorrow — today a bellyful, tomorrow a fight, and the day after God knows what! I have no quarrel with the law of destiny!"

I may have felt like a man on a wild-goose chase. In fact, I know I did. But you couldn't for the life of you escape the spirit of the game; and even with bones and muscles sore from Mujrim's racking, and a cut in the calf of my leg that was beginning to smart unmercifully as it grew stiff and the hot wind dried the bandage, I felt about as merry as the rest did.

THAT Valley of Moses is as savage and as endless as the Khyber; but we emerged from it at last into a waste of hot rock, deep *wadi* [ravine or valley], and oleander scrub, with rounded, rolling foothills all about us, and in places great heaps of human bones all cracked up by the jackals — bones, I dare say, of the Turkish soldiers who had tried to turn Lawrence out of Petra during the great war, the skulls persisting, as usual, long after the other bones had lost their shape. I wonder why a man's rib-bones disappear first. Has it anything to do with Eve?

Grim called never another halt until near evening, when we found a thing they call a *fiumara,* which is a dried-up watercourse that winds between hills and widens until it reaches the sea. There isn't any one word in the English language that translates it, nor for that matter any exactly similar formation elsewhere. Excepting for a week or two in odd seasons of heavy rain they use those *fiumaras* as roads and camping-places, their winding habit suiting the Bedouin's wandering taste, and the curves between high banks providing shelter both from hot wind and observation.

Our protesting camels — they always protest at down-hill work — stumbled into the *fiumara* at a point where a peculiar, flat-topped island split the course in two and storm-water had hollowed out a deep, curving cliff in the near bank. It was a fine place to camp in, for there were three deep holes in the bed of the *fiumara* with two or three feet of dirty water in the bottom of them; and, in a land where no Bedouin will lead you to water at any price, stuff of the color of soup and the flavor of stale cabbage is a great discovery. Besides, the camels like it better than the sort that bubbles from a clear spring; and after all, the animal that carries you in the teeth of the *simuum* [hot wind] deserves to be considered first.

The tents were pitched in a jiffy, for everybody craved sleep, and there seemed to be a pretty general impression that whoever could hurry first into the land of dreams would be considered unfit for guard duty when Grim should get around to making his selections. But I glanced at Narayan Singh, and Narayan Singh smiled at me; we both knew Grim by that time. He doesn't find soft billets for his friends when the watch needs keeping, any more than the wise banker pledges questionable credits.

So the mess of dates and rice was hardly eaten before the tents resounded with snores, those who were not yet really asleep pretending to be with all the more fervor. But as the moon rose over the rim of the hills of Edom, Grim called a conference of Jael Higg, Narayan Singh, himself and me, up on the flat-topped island, from which we had a fair view in the mellow moonlight of most of the country round about for a radius of nearly a mile.

The desert reflected so much of the moon's rays that at a hundred yards you could actually distinguish the tufts of hair and markings on a scavenging hyena. But down in the hollow where the tents were, all was dark.

We sat facing, in a square, on prayer mats. Jael Higg at first could hardly keep awake; but hers was the kind of intellect that drives its owner weasel-fashion, and it did not take a dozen words to make her forget sleep.

"Now, Jael," Grim began, and I have heard a doctor lecturing in just the same tone of voice a patient who can pull through if he will hear and use horse sense, "we're within five miles of the place where we're to pick up Ali Higg's hundred and forty men. Twenty miles farther to the south of that is the Avenger at Abu Lissan with eight hundred. If it comes to a fight you can guess as well as any one what our chance is worth. Something less than ten cents, eh?"

She nodded, every faculty alert. I rather liked her just then, for she was brave, whatever conventions she had broken. I know how necessary some conventions are, but Lord! I do admire courage in man or woman; and I never worry much about another fellow's morals, having all my work cut out to manage my own. I have met many a worse and more merciless woman than Jael Higg in what is called civilized society.

"You understand, don't you?" Grim went on. "I'm not interested in destroying you and Ali Higg. If the Arabs hereabouts would like you two for rulers, that's their affair. I'll not prevent that. I'm hired by the British to help keep the peace. They couldn't hire me for any other purpose. I want to see Arabia rule itself. That's my particular bug.

"It's too late to argue whether I'm right or wrong. We're facing facts. I'm Hell-bent on just that. And the Arabs haven't a chance unless they quit cutting up — not one chance in a hundred million.

"I happen to know that the British don't want to come over here and govern this country, for one reason because they can't afford it; but you all are busy fixing it so they'll have to come, because they can afford still less to have a constant state of war along their border. D'you get me?"

She nodded again — hard-eyed. She understood him perfectly. What most altruists don't understand is that the people they would benefit rather resent it than otherwise, and after profiting as much as possible intend to ditch them at the first chance. But Grim knew all about that.

"I don't pretend to know what's going on in your mind," Grim continued. "But supposing I were you, and you were I, it may be I might feel revengeful. I might think in that case that outside interference of any sort was impertinence to be punished without gloves.

"But, you see, you're a foreigner, too, Jael; you're from the Balkans, with a New York education; and Ali Higg's from the south of Arabia, which is a mighty long way off, so he's as good as a foreigner in the bargain. So I guess, as far as impertinence goes, the lot of us are in one boat. Let's call that account balanced, and draw a line under it.

"Then there's the personal side of it, and that's not so easy to argue about. I never met any one of spirit who enjoyed to take a defeat sitting. You've got spirit, and so has that husband of yours, and I can figure how you both feel. I'm sure sorry to hurt anybody's feelings. I know, when any of these brass hats in Jerusalem puts one over on me, I feel mad all through.

"There've been occasions when I've watched my chance and got even, with a shade the advantage by way of compound interest. That's human. And I'm pretty sure you'd like to knock the props from under me. Well, you're going to get the chance tomorrow morning."

Her thin lips quivered into a smile. It was frank, too; there was nothing furtive about it. You couldn't rightly call her treacherous, because she didn't pretend to be other than an enemy, seeking her own advantage in every circumstance. But she was longer-sighted than the Lion of Petra, and, having lived in America, understood something of the theory, at any rate, of giving the under-dog a chance. She knew enough to know Grim wasn't setting traps for her.

"D'you mean you expect me to kiss and be friends?" she answered.

"Bah! I gave you that chance once. I offered to put you into Ali Higg's shoes, and you refused it.

"Now you think my position is beginning to be stronger than it was, with a hundred and forty men almost within reach, and you plan to make terms. Thanks! I think I realize the strength of my position, too."

"I guess I'll have to disillusion you," said Grim. "You think your men will have captured Yussuf and that the order on the bank for fifty thousand pounds will be safely torn up or burned tomorrow morning. You'll have to guess again.

"I don't care how much money you gave my man Ali Baba; it wasn't enough. He had orders from me to accept any bribery you might give him, and to destroy in the desert whatever secret message you might send to Ibrahim ben Ah.

"So, you see, the men in the oasis weren't on the lookout for Yussuf after all, and it's a safe bet that he got through. So we're just where we left off, aren't we? If you should turn on me — as you might, and scupper my outfit — as is just possible, you'd lose that fifty thousand, Jael, to say nothing of being bombed out of Petra by aeroplanes. Now — are we clear on that point?"

"Well? What then?" she answered in a dry voice.

Grim had played the hand well. He had finessed the trick. She hadn't a trump left, or so she seemed to admit.

"Why — hadn't you better sit into the game and help me euchre this Avenger person, rather than spoil the game for every one, yourself included? I'm going to put you in charge of the hundred and forty men tomorrow morning."

"Whether I promise or not?"

"Sure. What is your bare promise worth to me? You're woman of the world enough to know I'm playing square; and you've got too much sense to suppose I'd trust you without some sort of guarantee. I've kind o' proved that, haven't I, by making you give that order on the bank?"

"Well, what more guarantee d'you want?" she demanded tartly.

"None, except — you keep on saying I don't know on which side my bread's buttered — I'll feel safer when I'm sure you know where the grease collides with your piece. Once you understand thoroughly that I'm out to see you score off the Avenger person, and that if you put a stick in my wheel you'll be stalling your own wagon, you and I are going to pull together right well."

At that Narayan Singh saw fit to lend his counsel.

"All well and good, Jimgrim *Sahib*; but let me go with her. She knows you for a man of peace, who hates to inconvenience a woman; but me she knows for a Pathan, to whom it would be small inconvenience, and in certain circumstances quite amusing, to rid the earth of any enemy of yours.

"Send me with her, *sahib*. I will be the guarantee. Then if she plays you a trick there will be one more head in the world without a pair of shoulders under it."

Jael Higg laughed outright at that, and I think she was really amused at the notion of anybody acting as a check on her if Grim should let her go. "Did you ever see a lamb act jailer to a she-wolf?" she asked; and at that it was the Sikh's turn to roar with laughter.

"Man, woman or child, you are the first who called me a lamb!" he answered. "Blood of Allah, but that is a good one!"

Like most Sikhs, he thoroughly despises the Moslem creed, and made up for having to pretend to be a follower of the Prophet by using the most atrocious oaths. They set even Jael Higg's teeth on edge, and she was no mealy-mouthed Puritan.

"I'll set no watch on you, Jael," Grim went on. "It's up to you whether you ride straight or not. My game must be pretty obvious. I'm going to pretend I'm Ali Higg. Ibrahim ben Ah, or any of those hundred and forty, would detect me in a second if they saw me by daylight, or even at close quarters in the dark.

"So what I want you to do is to maneuver them according to orders that I'll send you by messenger from time to time. They're plenty used to obeying you, and there'll be no trouble if you're so minded. You'll bear me out that first and last I've done nothing to discredit you with Ali Higg, or your men either. Now which is it to be?"

"What's your plan?" she asked.

And I took that for a good sign. If she had intended treachery, she would almost certainly have agreed first and asked for particulars afterward.

"WE'VE got to make the Avenger person," said Jimgrim, "believe we're stronger than we are, and force a guarantee from him too. I guess you've never studied the Duke of Wellington? You'd better do it, Jael, if you hope to succeed at your business. He claimed that he beat Napoleon by not having cast-iron plans. He said, if I recall it right, that the plans of either side were like their mule-harness. Napoleon's mules were all turned out perfectly with fine, strong leather harness; but when the leather busted they couldn't fix it; and so with their plan of campaign.

"But the Iron Duke's mule-harness was all ropes and string; when any part gave out they tied a knot in it and went on. Same with his plan of campaign. Same with mine. I've got a good general idea of what to do, but it's no part of my method to spoil prospects by being too darned definite in advance.

"You see, if you've a tight-drawn plan the enemy can find it out and run a spike into it. I've got all this Abu Lissan country in my head, because one of my jobs during the war was to make a map of it. I'll pass you the word from time to time where to go, where to hide, where to show yourselves, and what to do next; and if you keep your men in hand I think I can guarantee there won't be one casualty."

"And you'll leave me free to return to Petra afterward?" asked Jael.

"Why not?"

"With all my men?"

"Sure, if they care to follow you."

"Very well," she answered. "You're a fool, James Grim, but I think you're honest. There's no such fool as an honest one! I'll play your game this once. But I give you warning. If you lose it, I'll leave you in the lurch; and if you win, that's the end of it and we cry quits. Thereafter if I ever get you in my power don't count on my forgiveness! You had your last chance of making a friend of me when you turned down my offer."

"Sure," he answered, "I can sympathize with your personal feelings."

"A cent for your sympathy!" she snapped and I think she was on the verge of tears, although she was too proud and too much a termagant to let them fall.

"Suppose you go and sleep, Jael," he suggested. "We'll all need our wits tomorrow morning."

She rose without answering, started for the stepping-stones that led down into the bed of the *fiumara*, and turned again suddenly.

"What about the woman Ayisha?" she demanded. "Am I to be saddled afterward with her? I warn you —"

Grim laughed and shook his head.

"I allow she'd be more nervous about that than you," he answered. "No. I won't saddle you with her. Good night, Jael."

She didn't answer, but dropped down into the darkness, finding her footing with the nimbleness and lack of hesitation that typified her mental qualities by which she had established a position in the desert.

As soon as she had gone Grim turned to Narayan Singh and me.

"It hardly seems fair, you fellows," he said, smiling. "You're as sleepy and tired as I am. But tomorrow I've got to have my brains awake or we'll all go fluey. You've got to stand watch tonight between you, and no argument. Better stay up here, where you can get a good view all around.

"My tent is that one beside the big boulder in the *fiumara* bed; if anything happens, don't yell, but throw rocks until I wake and come and join you. You'll be so all in by tomorrow that you'll be able to sleep on camel-back. Good night; I'm off!"

"Nevertheless, our Jimgrim has a plan all cut and dried," said Narayan Singh as soon as Grim was out of earshot. "Only, he knows that that she-wolf is the enemy, and will not risk telling her.

"Moreover, he said, 'stand watch between us.' There was nothing about being both awake at once.

"Have you a coin, *sahib*? I have only nine piasters, and the Prophet of these people couldn't tell the head from the tail of any one of them. Let us take four-hour watches, turn and turn, and toss to see who sleeps first."

"I'll toss you," said I, "but let's take half-hour turns. It's easier to keep awake for thirty minutes than four hours."

He agreed to that, so I spun a coin and won the first spell of sleep. Maybe I'm an expert. At the end of six or seven seconds he awoke me, and swore he had allowed me several minutes more than half an hour. Then he took a turn, and when I shook him awake he vowed I wasn't playing fair.

"Sleeping or waking, I know the length of a second and a half!" he grumbled.

But I showed him the watch. When he accused me of having moved the hands I showed him how the shadow of the moon had traveled, and demanded time out, in the bargain, to compensate for the minute we had wasted arguing. It was like a game of cat-naps.

All the same, however short the snatches of sleep seemed, I'm convinced that in circumstances like that short turns are always best. Anything may happen in the night, and it's better then that each should have slept a little than that one should have had four hours, say, and the other none. Events proved that I was right in that instance, anyhow.

CHAPTER V

"May you deal with your enemies like iron, even as you deal with me."

W E TOOK turns until midnight, when the moon, a day or two past full, was almost overhead, bathing the desert with honey-colored light in every direction. The desert is more full of night sounds than a forest if you listen intently enough, for the sand creeps musically and there is no rustling of trees to cover up the infinitely tiny noises of the lesser prowlers.

After ten minutes or so of sitting motionless a hyena becomes a lumbering rowdy, a jackal a clumsy clod-walloper, and a mouse seems to make as much noise as a man. But when a man moves, all is instant silence by comparison.

I was making the most of one of my short turns of sleep when Narayan Singh awoke me by the practical expedient of laying his right hand across my mouth. I deduced that he did not want me to swear out loud; so I bit his finger pretty sharply to prove I was awake, and lay and listened.

There was something moving sure enough, and it wasn't an animal. The sound was too irregular and stealthy for that of any creature with a right to be at large. It was a human, trying not to attract attention — than which there is nothing more compelling of attention in the whole wide world, unless you are one of those folk who live forever in cities with their ears and eyes shut.

As I lay I could see Narayan Singh sitting absolutely motionless, shrouded so as to look shapeless in his Bedouin cloak. I imagine he and I together might have been mistaken for a lump of rock unless either of us moved. And there are two tricks of moving that hunting teaches you; one is to do it suddenly and then be absolutely still again; the other is to change position so slowly that no eye, not deliberately measuring your outline against a fixed mark, can detect the motion.

If you know you are being watched the first is usually best, because if you are absolutely still again the moment afterward the watcher will doubt the evidence of his own eyes. But it needs practice. The one thing not to do is to change position in jerks, or moderately slowly.

You can't judge much from a superficial glance at such a veteran scout as Narayan Singh. He was facing pretty nearly due east; but that didn't mean he was looking in that direction. Almost the surest means of allaying the suspicion of man or animal is to seem to look another way. Most Sikhs are past-master experts at that.

I lay and studied Narayan Singh for about two minutes before I was sure he was watching something over to his left. And it was another two minutes before I made out the head of a kneeling camel protruding from behind a rock at about the farthest range of vision in that peculiar light. It might have been half a mile away, or less.

The rock was big enough to hide a dozen camels; so it seemed likely there were more behind it, because a man with only one camel, who wanted to conceal the beast, would have done the job thoroughly; whereas if there were more than one there the end one might have been crowded into view.

Almost all the way along, between the camel's head and the edge of the *fiumara,* there was a series of shadows cast by boulders and sand-heaps. They were short, because of the position of the moon, and considerably broken up; but they formed the only line which animal or man might hope to approach us from the direction of that camel unobserved. There were occasional gaps in the shadow of as much as twenty feet of glistening sand. It wasn't long before I made out a man's shape moving swiftly from one spot of shadow to the next.

He took his time in the shadows, kneeling down to crawl and becoming very difficult to see, but hurrying across the light after watching to make sure he was unobserved. The light was tricky, but I don't doubt I could have put a bullet through him by the time he came within a hundred yards or so.

However, there was no need. An occasional glance in the direction of that camel's head was sufficient to make sure that none of his friends was prowling our way too; and it seemed wiser to discover what he was up to, than to stop him.

But it wouldn't have done to try to arouse Grim. If one of us had moved to throw a rock at Grim's tent the man would certainly have seen us; and if we had called out loud enough to waken Grim the man would almost certainly have heard. We kept quite still, and let him come within twenty yards of the *fiumara.*

Then he lay prone on his belly, watched like a leopard for at least five minutes, examining every detail of the ground in front of him, and began to crawl closer, advancing a yard at a time and pausing to re-scrutinize each shadow. He did a pretty good job on the whole. If Narayan Singh were not a trained scout and I a hunter, he might very likely have reached our camp unseen.

At last he reached the sharp brim of the *fiumara,* thrust his head and shoulders over it, and peered down; and then it became a problem what to do with him. If we once let him get down into the black shadow below, the advantage would be all on his side. I could see the moonlight sheening on his long knife-blade.

He might be an assassin sent by Ali Higg to murder Grim; but that was doubtful, because he dragged along a rifle with him as well, and the midnight murderers of that land don't encumber themselves with long-range artillery that might get in their way in a scuffle and prevent escape. I judged he didn't mean to take chances down in the dark, and it turned out I was right.

He would have had two bullets in him the same instant if he had started down toward the tents, for Narayan Singh said afterward that he had formed the same judgment and decision that I did.

However, he lay there and barked like a jackal instead. It was very well done. The pests had been snarling and yapping all around us on and off ever since the moon rose, and unless some one had been listening for a signal, or actually watching him as we were, that bark would have got by as a normal night noise. It only differed from a genuine jackal's bark in its regularity; he made exactly the same succession of sounds four times at equal intervals — a thing a jackal never does.

And somebody was listening below for just that signal. There was no answer, but he evidently saw somebody move down there in the darkness, for he was satisfied and drew back his head and shoulders.

Because of our position in the middle of the island we couldn't see down into the *fiumara,* but we heard footsteps; and presently the man spoke and was answered. We could hear both voices, but both failed to catch the words, or to distinguish whether the voice below was man's or woman's.

However, we weren't long in doubt. A head that was unmistakably Ayisha's emerged above the edge of the bank, coming up the track our camels had used. The man spoke to her again, and crawled away toward a good-sized boulder to his left hand and our right, fifty yards off along the bank. She followed him, bolt upright, walking like a ghost. It takes a woman to ignore the possibilities that scare a man into all manner of precautions. They both disappeared behind the boulder. The single camel's head was still visible sticking out like a big snake's from behind the rock in the near distance, and there was no other sign of activity; so Narayan Singh and I dared to breathe normally at last, and speak in low tones.

"One of us should go close and listen to their talk, *sahib,*" said the Sikh. "Which of us shall it be?"

"Both of us," I answered. "You go ahead. I'll wake Jimgrim and follow."

A couple of points were obvious. Some one had followed us from Petra: for who else could have guessed Ayisha's whereabouts? She might have made arrangements with one of the Lion's junior wives or concubines to organize communications as soon as possible after our backs were turned; I was absolutely positive that she had answered a prearranged signal. The other point was that Grim could keep watch on top of the island and be in the best position from which to issue orders, at one and the same time.

So I crept down quietly behind Narayan Singh, and threw a handful of small rocks on Grim's tent at short range. He would probably have fired at me if I had used any other means of waking him, because, seeing we had arranged the proper signal, he would naturally suppose any one entering his tent quietly to be an enemy; and I would have had to go quietly for fear of arousing the camp, whose noise would then have disturbed Ayisha. To cut short her interview with that night prowler might mean depriving Grim of valuable information.

As SOON as Jimgrim thrust his head out of the tent I told him what was happening. He went at once to the top of the island, and I started after Narayan Singh. There wasn't a sign of the Sikh by that time. I could still make out the camel's head in the distance, moving rhythmically as the beast belched and chewed its cud, but there was no trace of a human being anywhere; and, as it happened, our own camels were making quite a din just then, down in the *fiumara* — dreaming or something.

The brutes usually have bad dreams and let high heaven know it. Their guttural objections and shuffling were loud enough to drown any reasonable footfall, so I took the simplest course and walked straight forward, taking one sole precaution. The jingle of a rifle-swivel in the night can be safely guaranteed to wake the seven sleepers. I don't know why, but there's the fact. I've seen many a long stalk spoiled by it, and some men never learn.

By holding that loose swivel I actually stepped on Narayan Singh before he was aware of me, which says something for his skill in taking cover. He was lying in broad moonlight between two ridges of sand on the side of the boulder nearest the *fiumara,* too busy listening to make a sign of any sort to me; so I went round to the other side and crouched in the short shadow.

I judged the interview was pretty nearly over. The two were conversing in such low tones that you could hardly distinguish Ayisha's from the man's voice; but I heard her say —

"And is Jimgrim known so well to the Avenger?"

"Only by name," the man answered. "But the Lion knows no English," she retorted.

"*Wallahi!* Neither does the Avenger know a word of it."

"And Jael? Does she know of this?"

"Allah! Has the Lion a trick worth trying that she did not first whisper to him? It was she who thought of it."

"May Allah do so to me, and more, unless I drive a knife into her heart before tomorrow's sun sets!" hissed Ayisha. "Go now, or those two fat Indians on the rock will cease snoring and see us."

But the man would not go. He seemed to put a pretty high value on Jael's life. I heard him catch at Ayisha's garments as she started up to leave him, and although she cursed like a wet cat he wouldn't let go of her.

"Woman, if you kill Jael," he insisted, "that will be the end of all of us. Better by far slay the Lion himself. Jael is the real leader. We would all follow Jael if the Lion were dead."

"Into *jahannum* she would lead you!" Ayisha answered.

"That may be; for what is written shall come to pass. But better into *jahannum* behind her than to live here leaderless."

"Bah! Father of fear! There are other leaders."

"None fit to touch her garment. You must not kill her."

"That is my affair."

"I say you shall not."

"Son of sixty dogs, let go of me!"

She made a sound between a curse and a scream, as if some one had taken her by the throat, and I judged it time to interfere. It was just two strides around that end of the rock, and I beat Narayan Singh by half a second.

The man's long knife was drawn, and he had his fingers on her throat, as I had guessed. The butt of my rifle sent the knife spinning, the Sikh dragged Ayisha away, and I rushed the fellow before he could draw a second knife.

He was lying on his back in an instant, with the weight of my big hams on his chest. Narayan Singh pounced on his rifle while I searched him diligently for hidden hardware, tossing them out one by one. When I was quite sure he hadn't any kind of weapon left I let him sit up and recover breath.

With his first wind he began to beg for liberty, vowing he had never harmed me, nor intended to.

"May your honor live forever!" he roared out; and I let him roar, for it didn't seem to matter now whether the whole camp was wakened or not.

Next he offered me a camel as the price of freedom. When I laughed at that, he swore he would pray for me three times daily for a year if I would let him go. He was dead set on getting away from us; he even offered me his rifle as a souvenir of the occasion. It was too bad to have to entertain such an awfully unwilling guest.

"Come on," I said, "and learn the worst. Perhaps you won't be beaten very badly."

At that he even offered to lie down and let me beat him — anything, in fact, if I would only let him go. On the whole I judged he might prove a pretty important capture, and as he wouldn't see sense I seized him at last by the scruff of his unwashed neck and forced him along in front of me. He hadn't strength enough to make me exert myself, but he struggled like a hooked eel all the way.

I felt like a New York cop running in a pickpocket, and the funniest part of it was that Narayan Singh strode along just in front, with his arm around Ayisha's shoulders, booming titanic love-stuff into her unwilling ears.

"What have I vowed a hundred times, beloved? Hah! If that had been an army hedged in with a sea of fire, I would have jumped the fire and freed you! What are bayonets and guns," he boomed, "to one who loves as I do?

"Come closer, Jewel of the Desert! Lean on your protector! We Pathans of the Orakzai have hairy arms, but they are strong to nestle in. Let me look into those liquid eyes and see how fairer they are than the moon and stars!"

"Father of pigs!" she retorted. "Get away from me. I choose to walk alone."

"Nay, beloved; come closer! One danger is enough to run for this night. Next we must face Jimgrim, and you need a protector from his wrath. He will accuse you of treachery while he slept.

"You must lean on me. You must depend on me to defend you. We Pathans of the Orakzai are wondrous liars. A man's sword and a man's tongue should be ready for any occasion, say we. Now put me to the test, O Heart of all Loveliness. What shall we tell Jimgrim?"

But though he called her by a fabulous long string of jeweled names, offered her the hills of Edom for a kingdom and the fairest cities of the earth for plunder, he could get no answer out of her at all, until we came to the brim of the *fiumara* and were challenged by three separate members of our startled camp. We had to answer the challenge right swiftly, for the click of rifle-bolts preceded it.

Then Narayan Singh took Ayisha by both arms and swung her in front of him.

"Must I tell him all I heard?" he asked. "Oh, Heart's Delight, don't put me to that necessity!"

"Black pig! Let go of me!"

But he held on, and my prisoner — no more aware than I was that the Sikh had not been able to hear the first part of the conversation at all — piped up in support of him.

"I have a tale I shall tell," he announced. "Listen, Lady Ayisha, this great fellow is a friend of yours. Humor him. He is willing to stand between us and this Jimgrim. Better let me tell the tale, and you confirm what I say. None ever believes a woman, but he will believe me."

At that Narayan Singh laughed gruffly, and I detected a note of triumph, although he affected defeat.

"Malaish [No matter]," he said with a shrug of his great shoulders and loosing Ayisha's arms; "there is nothing for it but to tell the truth. I shall tell Jimgrim every word I overheard from first to last."

He had gained his point. Ayisha made up her mind that he had heard everything, and whatever her first intention might have been she decided now to make a virtue of necessity.

"I need no ignorant Pathan to speak for me!" she retorted. "It is I, not you, who will tell him. Get behind me, son of sixty dogs!"

But instead of obeying that command he laughed aloud, picked her up like a child, and carried her down the dark track into the *fiumara*. She didn't seem to mind that part of it. In fact, one of the most surprising things anywhere east of, say, the North Sea is the complaisance with which women submit to being seized and carried off.

He carried her straight up to Grim, and set her on her feet in front of him on top of the island, and I think that by the time she got that far her private opinion of the Sikh had undergone considerable modification.

I SENT my prisoner up between two of our Arabs, and went to have a quiet look at Jael's tent. There wasn't a sound. I hardly cared to open the fly and look in, so I counted the camels. The Bishareen dromedary wasn't there.

I returned to her tent, and this time didn't hesitate to peer inside. It was empty. The sheepskin rug and blankets were gone too.

Several of our Arabs were still asleep among the camels; it wouldn't have been the slightest use to arouse and question them. The remainder had slept until my prisoner's bellowing disturbed them, and wouldn't believe me at first when I said the Bishareen was gone. I went up to Grim with the bad news, but he was aware of it already.

"There she goes," he said before I could begin to tell him.

He nodded toward the northeast. The little Bishareen was eating stick and galloping at top speed in the direction of the rock from behind which Ayisha's visitor had come — silhouetted softly in the moonlight just out of reasonable rifle-shot. It looked exactly like one of those up-to-the-minute motion pictures, especially as there was too much noise in our camp by that time for us to hear the camel's footfall. Most of our men were clambering out of the *fiumara* and shouting to Grim to know whether they should open fire or not. He shouted to them to do nothing.

What Jael had accomplished looked remarkably like a miracle to me. It was obvious, of course, now why the camels had been making all that noise when I started to follow Narayan Singh. But how in the world she had saddled that beast and got away without disturbing the men who slept by the picket stakes was the mystery, unless there was a traitor in our camp. The saddle alone was as much as most women could lift.

She must have chosen the exact moment when Grim and I were both engaged in climbing out of the river-bed, he in one direction, I in the other, to start up the *fiumara* and disappear around the nearest bend. The rest would be easy enough; no doubt there were plenty of places higher up where a camel could find footing and negotiate the bank.

We hadn't a beast in camp that could overtake that Bishareen. It could go like the wind, and Jael was about half the weight of anybody we could mount and send in pursuit of her. So unless Grim chose to try long-range shooting by moonlight, which in ninety-nine percent of cases is a useless waste of ammunition, there was nothing much to do but watch.

She headed straight for that big rock, from behind which a camel's head still protruded, and presently disappeared.

"Now," said Grim, "what's the excitement all about?"

He looked cheerful enough to have planned the whole business.

Ayisha squatted down comfortably in front of him, giving the rest of us a good view of her back. That trick is part of a woman's language; no male could ever contrive it in exactly the same way, suggesting indisputable superiority of intellect, class, knowledge, opportunity, privilege and everything. Grim waited for her to speak first, and she kept him waiting, while my prisoner trembled in his skin and Narayan Singh stroked his great beard upward with both hands.

"O Jimgrim," she said at last, "you would better make an end of foolishness and marry me."

Nobody gasped. Nobody cracked a smile — least of all Grim. There wasn't really anything to smile about, considering time, place and circumstances. History was merely repeating itself. For the hundred-millionth time a female of the species considered that a man was captive of her bow and spear, and the member of the less conventional sex was trying to make the most of opportunity.

"Why, O Lady Ayisha?" Grim asked her blandly.

"Am I not fair to look at? This Pathan of yours vows I am fairer than the moon and stars. He ought to know, for he has loved many women in many lands."

"*Shellabi kabir!* [Extremely beautiful!]" Grim answered. "The fellow flattered stars and moon by speaking of them in the same breath. Yet the Prophet said, Ayisha, that the houris wait for us in paradise. Who should anticipate the joys of that world in the make-belief of this?"

"Yet the Prophet did!" she answered. "He had many wives."

"Truly, but then he was a prophet," Grim replied. "Can you tell me why I should pause in the midst of happenings to make a marriage? There are twenty lives depending on my judgment. A mistake, a false move, and these friends of mine are dead men."

"Father of wise answers, that is why you must marry me," she answered. "No man can find his way out of the net a clever woman weaves. Jael has you in the toils. You need me, I tell you, to help you out of them."

"It seems, though, that you are not too far away just now to help me if you will," he suggested.

"*Inshallah,* if you marry me now, I will help you indeed," she answered. "You shall rule this country."

That was two women within a day who had proposed to make a king of him. Wouldn't you have felt tickled? I know I would, although nobody ever made me the proposal. Bearing in mind Narayan Singh's method of making love, and allowing a good margin for Eastern hyperbole in general, there was still much more than random flattery in the offer.

There are some men who can lead people — who can understand an alien race, deserve their allegiance and lift them toward progress. Grim undoubtedly had that gift. And how many exceptions are there

Jimgrim and the Woman Ayisha

to the rule in such cases that women have been first to recognize the fact, and to egg the man on in spite of himself? But Grim has less personal vanity than any man I know, as well as a business instinct for appraising facts in all their bearings.

" 'Between the promise and the deed a man may marry off his ugly daughter,' " he quoted, using the famous Arab proverb. "Tell me what you know and I will listen."

"You are at Jael's mercy," she said, "unless you consent to be guided by me."

"How then?"

"You gave her too much opportunity. You let her talk with Ali Higg. You left them alone together. Then, like one who has set match to gunpowder, you came away, knowing nothing of what the fire said to the powder. But I listened, and I heard a little. And what I did not hear, another heard; and this shivering fool came in the night, bringing me word of it."

"I listen, O Lady Ayisha," said Grim.

"As a man to a tale that is told between waking and sleeping, or as a man to his wife, do you listen?"

"I have but one pair of ears," Grim answered.

"Aye, that listen to the she-wolf Jael!"

"That listen to all voices, whoever speaks. Who am I that should bury my head in the sand like an ostrich?"

She held her tongue for a full minute, while an owl hooted weirdly in the darkness up the *fiumara*. Then —

"Unless I speak you are ruined," she said at last.

Grim considered it his turn to wait. He simply watched her face with interest. The rest of us hardly breathed. At the end of a minute, since he made no suggestion:

"What if I do not speak?" she asked. "And what if I do?"

"If you do not, you are not my friend."

"And?"

"I have other friends," he answered calmly.

"None like me," she retorted.

"Truly. My other friends drive no hard bargains before they consent to tell me what they know."

Maybe Ayisha had forgotten Narayan Singh; more extraordinary things than that have happened in the strain of concentration. There was a general once who forgot an army corps. Or perhaps she thought he was so enamored of her that he would hold his tongue. At any rate, she ignored him, which was easy enough while he stood alongside me behind her.

But he bulks big in any kind of light, and she could not pretend not to see him when he strode around behind Grim and stood there facing her, with folded arms and his eyes fixed on her face. He said nothing. He didn't even cough to draw attention to himself. But it was an ultimatum, and she realized it.

I half-suspected by that time that the Sikh was bluffing. It seemed to me that if he had really overheard all that she said to my prisoner, and that the prisoner had said to her, Narayan Singh would have helped Grim out of a predicament and saved time by telling all he knew at once. But if she, too, suspected he was bluffing, she didn't dare challenge him.

"May you deal with your enemies like iron, even as you deal with me," she said to Grim at last. "Behold, it is the way of men to devour the women's harvest; and the women plant again, and reap again, and grind again, that their lords may eat. I will tell all; then, like all women, I will desire my lord's favor."

I COULD see the milk-white of Narayan Singh's teeth in the midst of his black beard, but if she saw the smile too, she pretended not to notice it. Grim merely nodded to her to continue.

"In the cave in Petra Jael said to Ali Higg:

" 'Behold, this fellow comes in your guise, letting men believe that he is the Lion of Petra. By a trick he has worsted you, for he is very cunning. In your name he will go against the Avenger, and it is well to let him go, for because of his cunning he will be too much for the Avenger, and will bring him to terms likewise. Thereafter both you and the Avenger will be as strong men bound, and this Jimgrim will be reckoned a great one. Like honey in his mouth is the success he tastes already. But is honey sweet only to the bees?' "

My prisoner was in as abject terror as I have ever known a man to be. I had my leg against him, so as to be aware of any movement he might make, and he was shivering as if he had the ague. I expect he was thinking of what Ali Higg would do to him if it ever transpired that he had helped betray the Lion's plans.

Grim nodded again, and Ayisha went on with her story.

"Ali Higg was unwilling to be urged into action, because his neck is sore; and besides he is ever opposed to Jael's plans at first, although always yielding to her finally. He said: 'Let him go against the Avenger. Who am I that should complain when Allah sends me aid? Can I overcome the Avenger without help? This Jimgrim, as you say, is cunning, and I shall reap the fruit of his cunning, and all will be well.'

"But she answered:

" 'Fool! Not thou, but he will reap. Who labors for other than his own reward? Hast thou ruled in Petra all these months, to believe yet that men risk their lives for the love of it, or for the love of thee?

" 'Consider now: There are three parties to this — thou, this Jimgrim, and the Avenger. Whose is the advantage to begin with? The Avenger's! And whose is the disadvantage? Thine!

" 'But this Jimgrim has taken on himself thy part. Take thou then his part. Jimgrim is the Lion. Let the Lion be Jimgrim. A sheep in the skin of a lion; a lion pretending to be a sheep! He has twenty men in all. Go thou abroad with twenty.' "

Ayisha paused dramatically to give her revelation time to take effect. In lands where almost no men, and even fewer women, can read, the art of reporting orally maintains a high plane. She waited for Grim to nod once more before resuming.

"Ali Higg was doubtful and afraid. He complained about his neck. He feared to leave Petra ungoverned. But she told him to cover up his neck with bandages, and to hide the bandages beneath the *kuffiyi* [headdress].

"He said he knew no English, and therefore could not pretend to be Jimgrim. But she said:

" 'Neither does the Avenger or any of his men know English; and is not Jimgrim pretending to be an Arab? Can not an Arab pretend to be an Arab likewise?'

"So he said again that if Petra were left ungoverned there would be no knowing what might happen. And she said:

" 'Then I myself will return and govern Petra. I will go with this Jimgrim, and make believe to fall in with his plans, displaying reluctance for the sake of being all the more convincing when I yield; but I will seize the first chance to escape and return to Petra, and occupy thy place until thou come again.'

"So spake Jael, and the Lion finally agreed."

She paused, and Grim spoke at last.

"Do she and the Lion still propose to let me deal with the Avenger?"

"Surely. And to defeat you afterward."

"Then who do they think will make Ibrahim ben Ah and his hundred and forty men obey me, seeing that Jael was to have contrived that part?"

"The Lion thought of that at once," Ayisha answered. "But Jael said:

" 'Malaish [No matter]. This Jimgrim thinks himself so clever. Let him puzzle out that problem after I have left him. If he finds a way, well and good. If not, we shall be no worse off, and an intruder will have burned his fingers. If Ibrahim ben Ah should suspect him, and lay hands on him, and kill him, let that be the judgment of Allah, and we will find another way to deal with the Avenger.' "

"And has Ali Higg left Petra?"

"Surely."

"And that camel yonder, whose head appeared just now from behind the rock?"

"There were three camels. This man came with two others to bring word to me. Jael knew nothing of that, but she will know now. That is why this man is afraid. But as the other two came to protect this one, and knew nothing, it may be they will tell her nothing; and this man, who is a father of lies always, can tell Jael that the Lion sent him to help her escape. So he has no need to feel so very much afraid, although he is a great coward."

Grim raised his eyebrows comically. It was a predicament all right.

CHAPTER VI

"I will stick that pig Yussuf when I find him!"

THE news spread through our camp on a twinkling, for the two men whom I had sent up to Grim with the prisoner while I looked into Jael's tent had been listening to Ayisha's story, and one of them ran down below to tell his brothers.

From their viewpoint it was a wonder of a tale, full of enchanting possibilities and side issues, and especially gratifying because it would oblige Grim to display his genius for counter-intrigue. Their faith in him was measureless, and why not? Had he not outwitted Ali Baba, grandsire of the gang, and bound the whole lot by good-will to his chariot wheels? The man who could accomplish that was capable of anything. We could hear them down in the dark *fiumara* exclaiming: "Allah!" — *"Mashallah!"* — *"Mallahi!"* as the tale unfolded and its ramifications dawned on their appreciative minds.

It was no use my trying to suggest anything. I'm no diplomatist, and even strategy is a thing I can appreciate far better than invent. I suppose if we all were strategists it would take a man from Mars with something new, like "relativity," to lead us anywhere; and if we were all just plain Merry Andrews with a pound or two of muscle on our arms and legs, we'd reduce the world to a fine mess of hash. Each man to his profession, then, and let the man whose job is thinking have a chance to think.

Narayan Singh stood like a statue, making no sign. Grim sat looking at Ayisha, and the prisoner still trembled against my leg, although not so violently. Suddenly Grim pointed a finger at him.

"Go!" he ordered. "Give him back his weapons, somebody."

A startled cat would have taken longer to obey that order. Inside a minute the fellow was scrambling up the far bank of the *fiumara,* pursued by volleys of ridicule from our men. He wasted no time taking cover as he ran, but raced his own shadow across the open to the place where he had left his camel.

Ayisha with her placid brow and burning eyes had been doing some thinking meanwhile on her own account. She spoke at last — to Grim, of course; Narayan Singh and I hardly figured any longer in her consciousness.

"So now I have told all the truth. Am I unworthy of my lord's favor? I am as one who had a fortune and has given all of it. Shall I be cast off like a broken shoe?"

Grim seemed to come out of a brown study suddenly, and Narayan Singh heaved an enormous sigh of relief. I believe he had been praying to all the gods of the Hindu pantheon to give his leader wisdom; for he forgets his Sikhism in times of stress and falls from orthodoxy, speculating that there might be virtue in the old gods after all.

"There is no way, is there, by which Ibrahim ben Ah could have learned of your divorce?" Grim asked suddenly.

"Not unless old Ali Baba has told him," Ayisha answered.

"When that old fox parts with information he isn't paid for, it will be time for Gabriel to sound the last trump," Grim said, smiling. "Have you ever given orders to Ibrahim ben Ah, Ayisha?"

"A hundred times. I was the Lion's second wife. Once, when Jael was away with the Lion on a raid against the men of El-Kerak, I was left in sole command in Petra, with Ibrahim ben Ah and fifty men to do my bidding. I am a sheikh's oldest daughter," she added proudly. "I am used to being obeyed."

"And will you help me now?" Grim asked her.

"Even unto the end of the world," she answered in a voice that would have melted icebergs.

Her promise was likely more reliable than Jael Higg's, but she made it clear she would demand her price. It was difficult to guess whether she was really in love with Grim; not because he wasn't lovable from a woman's viewpoint, for at least a score of women of his own speech, and several from his own country, have made small secret of their regard for him. But the customs of the country entered into it.

Where women are practically bought and sold — occasionally given by their parents — and very often plundered like raided cattle, the sex acquires a viewpoint that the West can't grasp. The famous advice of the Quaker to his son, not to love money, but to love where money is, has its adaptation in Arabia; and it might be that Grim's peculiar genius pointed the way to her ambition.

Whether she would be really heart-broken in our sense of the word when the inevitable truth should dawn that Grim lived in another world, as it were, and never would dream of making her his wife, was a conundrum. Of one thing, though, I was certain: He would never be able to explain his reason to her. She was a sheikh's daughter — a princess of the pathless desert, fit to marry any one. The fact that her father lived in a goat-hair tent with several wives had nothing at all to do with it. However, that was Grim's problem, or perhaps Narayan Singh's; certainly not mine.

Grim told her to go to her tent, and she obeyed him as meekly as Ruth obeyed Boaz. I thought he was going to talk things over with the Sikh and me, but after another minute's silence he dismissed us as well.

"I've had all the sleep I need," he said. "I think I'll keep watch up here and puzzle out the workings of this mix-up. Suppose you fellows turn in down below there and make up for lost time. I guess I'll maybe need all your faculties when daylight comes."

So off we went, and turned in. It's mortifying in a way to be sent to bed like a small boy when your own life as likely as not hangs on the issue of deliberation. But there's nothing to be gained by intruding either your opinions or curiosity on a man who does his thinking best when undisturbed. I had a sort of nettled feeling that I'm not sure I wasn't entitled to, and that kept me from falling asleep for an hour.

After that Narayan Singh's snores made sleep impossible, until I put the heel of a tent-peg in his mouth. And even then the intermittent roars of laughter of our gang, who would wake one another to discuss some fresh angle of the situation, kept me from little more than dozing until nearly dawn. They seemed to consider that Ali Higg's turning the tables by masquerading as Jimgrim was the most prodigious joke that had ever been sprung on an amusing world.

When I left the tent at daybreak Grim was still sitting up there on the island, motionless, not even smoking. I went up at once, to find out whether he had formed a plan.

"Well?" I asked.

"Yes," he said, "I think all's well. I'd like to pull up stakes and get a move on, but we've got to consider the camels; the silly fools have lain there all night long with good corn on mats beside them and haven't touched a mouthful. We've got to wait and let them eat."

"What after that?"

"I want you and Narayan Singh to scout ahead and get in touch with Ibrahim ben Ah. The best bet would be to find Ali Baba first, but that's too much like luck to happen. He's a shrewd old fox, and if he gets first sight of you he's dead sure to try to give Ibrahim ben Ah the slip and give you the news out of earshot.

"Next best after that would be for you to take his place with Ibrahim ben Ah, and let the old man come to me with information. Somehow or other I've got to know the exact state of mind of that army of Ali Higg's before we try the long chance."

"Which is?"

"To send Ayisha to command them."

I laughed.

"She'll be a safer bet than Jael ever was," said I, "as long as she thinks there's a chance of her becoming Mrs. Jimgrim."

But he smiled back like a chess-player who can see about nine moves ahead.

"Jael kids herself she's dangerous," he said. "But I allow she'll watch her step on account of her fifty thousand pounds. And the Lion will watch his for the same reason. Besides, I'm counting on that sore neck to take the pep out of him. Prospects aren't so gloomy.

"What do you say to our setting those camels an example? Is breakfast ready?"

"See here, James Schuyler Grim," I answered. You're a darned good man, and I like you, and all that. But suppose you come across for once. Narayan Singh is a soldier; he'll obey orders and ask no questions; but I'm neither built nor trained that way. Doesn't it seem to you like good sense to take me into confidence?"

"Haven't I?" he asked, raising his eyebrows in obviously genuine surprise. "Seems to me I've trusted you till it's become a kind of habit."

"Have I failed you," I retorted, "that you can't give me at least an outline of your plan now?"

"Oh, is that the trouble?"

He seemed suddenly relieved.

"Why, no; that doesn't seem like sense to me. My plan might be no good. If that's so, I can change it. But if I tell it to you now, you're going to bear it in mind, and if any unforeseen contingency crops up you're going to be governed by the plan I outlined and maybe act in some way so that I shall have to follow up — which might be mighty inconvenient.

"But as long as you don't know what I'm contemplating you're not limited by it, any more than I'm limited by having to consult you before making a sudden change. We'd be like two fellows trying to play one poker hand."

"I should think you could give me a general idea."

"The general idea is to get in touch with the Avenger now and bluff him."

"I know that, of course. But along what line? What general principle?"

"I wonder if you'd mind not pressing that?" he answered. "Let's have this clear. It isn't you I don't trust, it's myself. The thought that I wasn't absolutely free at any minute to turn my whole plan bottomside up, or discard it and try another one, would rattle me so I'd make mistakes.

"I haven't a secret you can't know; but I hate to tell a man something I don't know for sure; I'd feel sort of weak and helpless afterward. It's my fault, not yours; I'm built that way. If it isn't doing right by you, I beg pardon and ask you to be tolerant."

Well, I don't know that I liked it any better at the time, but I saw his point. I have got so since that I never think of pinning him down to an outline of his plan in any undertakings; and the method works well, although — and perhaps because — it calls for every ounce of zeal. You're on the jump the whole time. Not knowing what he's going to do next, you're like an infielder with three on bases.

But he has to choose his men discreetly. There are plenty of men more useful than myself, for instance, who wouldn't stand his reticence for a day. On the other hand, I never knew a man less prone to find fault than he is, or one more superbly tolerant of others' shortcomings.

A LITTLE more than an hour after dawn, while the desert was still cool, Narayan Singh and I set off together on the two best camels. I don't doubt I was still humping a grouch, and Narayan Singh divined the reason of it.

"By the bones in these hills," he laughed, "this is better sport than serving with the army, *sahib!* A soldier in the ranks such as I have ever been, and such as I am like to be again, unless our fate overtakes us all on this adventure, is told nothing — knows nothing — is nothing. He obeys. If a fool of an officer marches him face first into Hell, there is not even the satisfaction of a sort of explanation.

"Scouting for the army is rather better fun; but it is very little that a man finds out, and oftener than not that little is ignored; at the best, that one little scrap of information is but added to the mass like a grain of sand into a bushel of the stuff. Neither may a man scout as he would like to, but only as another wills. Whereas with Jimgrim —"

"Oh, shut up!" I growled. "I'm not here to be preached at."

"In an army, *sahib,* there would be much damning and very little preaching," he answered. "Whereas with Jimgrim, though he tells us precious little, we are free like hounds to draw the coverts for him, and there is neither leash nor whip.

"*Il hamdul illah,* as these heathen say, that Jimgrim is a prince of huntsmen, who knows when a good hound bays on a true scent. But an army had too many huntsmen, who talk among themselves, saying, 'Yes, sir, No, sir,' and then command the pack with a: 'Lo! The General Staff decrees that the scent lies yonder in that direction; therefore make haste to find it and bark loud!'

"This Jimgrim would have been a king if his mother had borne him on this side of the Atlantic. Are there others like him in America?"

Well, I grew good-tempered gradually, if for no other reason than because it was absurd to find fault with a man who could arouse such enthusiasm in a follower. Besides, I like Grim; and it's one of my fundamental articles of marrow-bone religion that if I'm a man's friend he may get away with anything except black treason. But leaving all that out of the reckoning, I defy any man to start off in the morning on a camel alongside Narayan Singh, with friends behind and the unknown just beyond the shimmering horizon, and retain a grouch for twenty minutes.

The hot wind wasn't due for an hour or two. The wound made by Ayisha's dagger in my leg didn't hurt more than was tolerable. The camels were feeling the effects of good corn and thorn-twigs, and went swinging along as if their legs were hung on springs. As long as you haven't got to spend your whole life in the desert, it's about the easiest of all earth's wonders to admire; and the secret of contentment lies in everlastingly admiring something — or so I've found it.

The Sikh began singing some sort of hymn set to minor music; and, though singing in the Jat-Punjabi dialect is one of those accomplishments that were omitted when my kit was tossed out of the great Quartermaster's store, I've always found a curious satisfaction, akin to inspiration, in listening to songs in the vernacular of other lands. Indian lyrics always seem to lose the note of plaintiveness when you translate them, just as Homer's verses lose their roll done into English, and the odes of Horace forced into another tongue come through without their humor:

> In the hot night my mother bore me,
> Knowing not who I am!
> Into the dawn I came, a man-child,
> Knowing not the life before me,
> Stranger to the folk about me.
> None knew who I am!
> Out of the book of signs and wonders,
> Knowing not who I am,
> Soothsayers read this and that thing.
> There is lightning when it thunders;
> Do they know the lightning's *karma*?
> None knew who I am!
> Out of her heart my mother taught me
> (Stranger, nevertheless!)
> Fear and faith and law and legend,
> Weeping when my *karma* caught me
> Willing yet unwilling — tore me
> Loose from her caress.
> Smiled the Powers then at the stripling
> Facing first duress,
> Making boast of all that might be,
> Choosing pleasant ways and crippling
> Choice for sake of this or that one
> (Strangers, nevertheless!)
> Thrice and again my *karma* took me
> (None knew who I am!)
> Rolling me in red disaster
> Till the light o' loves forsook me
> And I cried to careless heavens,
> Asking who I am!
> Long were the nights I spent in anguish,
> Thinking gods would care,
> Vowing I myself would hardly
> Leave a thing I made to languish;
> If I perished who would profit,
> How, and when, and where?
> Then I struck a rock, demanding
> Why it towered there,
> And, as if the rock made answer,
> Dawned upon my understanding
> "That is His affair!"
> Then I looked from rock and river
> To horizon far,
> Eying with a new contentment,
> Seeing gifts but not the Giver,

Sun and moon and star,
Stream and forest, time and season,
Fish and bird and beast and man;
None could look into their reason,
None knew what they are!
So there burst illumination
Dissipating fears,
And I sang a song of manhood,
And I laughed at the negation
That is affluent of tears,
Is the sun too long a-borning?
Are the planets in arrears?
Who am I? Whoever knows me
Is the Monarch of the Morning,
Is the Lord of love and laughter,
Is the Owner of the years!

You hardly expect a sporadically dissolute enlisted Sikh to sing that kind of song. But, as the missionaries say, the Sikhs are heathen, and on their way to Hell; so we, who don't believe that laughter and religion and the morning are all one, and who think we know exactly who we are, mustn't judge them too harshly.

Personally I'm not much of a dogmatist. Having pitched my tent in Hades a lot of times, I'm not so scared as I used to be. And if there's a worse Hell than I've camped in yet, as long as there are Sikhs there like Narayan Singh I don't believe I'm going to worry much. They'll sing songs, and we'll find a way out somehow.

I have told only part of Narayan Singh's song that he trolled that morning in a rather nasal baritone, because the censor would object to about two-thirds of it. The East is peculiarly frank in some matters that the West prefers to keep behind a veil of mystery, and there were details concerning lights o' love that were interesting, whatever else they might be.

I got to thinking about India, and the fact, admitting of no dispute, that during all the uncontrollable deviltry of the Indian Mutiny of '57 there wasn't a single instance of mistreatment of an Englishwoman by the sepoys. So I asked him about Ayisha, wondering just how far he proposed to go with his mock love-making.

"Would she make a good wife for a soldier?" I suggested.

To my surprise, instead of laughing he meditated for several minutes before answering. Then: "The world has this marriage business upside down," he said at last. "A woman is either ambitious, and drives a man as Jael drives the Lion of Petra; or else she is a parasite, who halves his joys and multiplies his sorrows. Single, she is sometimes a delight; married, she is torment.

"As for men: Well, *sahib,* our Jimgrim and you and I are single men. I have not heard him or you complain of it. Nor you me. I have nine piasters and my freedom; show me the woman that can rob me of either!"

But I was still curious. He had not told me yet what I wanted to know.

"She's in an awkward position," I said. "What do you suppose is in store for her?"

"Awkward? How so?" he answered. "At the mercy of our seventeen thieves, she would be a baggage to be bought and sold. But there are three of us who would not see her brought to a bad end. Ayisha is like all women; she thinks she has me at her feet, and so despises me, to my no small comfort. She despairs of Jimgrim, and therefore idolizes him, to his discomfort. And she has a woman's luck; for if I know anything, it is that Jimgrim will contrive good fortune for her."

"You think he's the executive of destiny?"

"All men are weapons in the hand of destiny. I am a sepoy — a number on a muster-roll; yet, counting all, I have slain in my day seven-and-thirty men with cold steel. Was that not destiny?

"I was born on the bank of the Jumna. I have killed men near the Ganges, near the Kabul River, near the Irrawaddy, near the Seine, near the Marne, near the Rhine — Pathans, Afghans, Hindus, Burmese, Prussians, Saxons, Austrians — having no personal quarrel with any one of them. And here, near the Jordan, I have slain two Syrians and an Egyptian — all with cold steel. Was that not destiny?

"And am I alone the tool of destiny? Each of us is like a pebble, *sahib,* dropped into a pool, causing rings of ripples that we can not check. I am not in the secret of destiny, but I know this: That our Jimgrim is causing a ripple that will set Ayisha on her feet."

"So you don't plan to make a ripple in her life?" I asked him.

"There is no need," he answered. "Besides, I am a man of few plans. My trade is obedience to orders; and as for amusement I ask no better than a day like this one, with not too many orders, and the unknown waiting to be considered, fifty or a hundred yards ahead."

Well, I don't want to be a, Sikh, but I can't beat that for philosophy.

The hot wind started and made further talk impossible with any degree of comfort, for we had to cover our faces. But he had given me plenty to think about, and the man who can't find entertainment in his own thoughts is in a bad way.

I suppose we rode three miles in silence — making eight or nine from our starting-point — before anything happened to break the desert spell. Then, in proof that reflection did not limit our faculties, we both spoke suddenly at once.

"*Dekko!*" said he.

"*Shuf!*" said I.

And we both meant the same thing —

"Look!"

MORE than a score of mounted camels were standing in a group on the horizon, cut off from us by a deep ravine that looked impassable. It seemed as if the men who rode them were holding a consultation; it was a fair guess that they had only just reached the spot. We halted and watched them.

After a minute or two they spread out into a long line, and began to come forward at a walk toward the ravine, constantly increasing the distance between them fanwise, as if scouting. But some of them were not very good scouts, or else the sun was too strong in their eyes, for it was quite a while before most of them saw us.

The first to spot us was a man near the middle of the line, but he made no signal to the others. I knew he had seen us, because he put on speed and slightly changed direction. He rode a nearly white camel — it looked all white at that distance.

"I would know that beast in a hundred thousand!" said Narayan Singh.

That was maybe an exaggeration. We have most of us known men who could pick one horse out of a mob infallibly at the first glance. I have seen cow-men do the same thing with a steer. But camels? Nevertheless, it did look like the Syrian beast that Ali Baba rode, and the action of its rider, forcing the pace, as he did, alone, did not quite suggest an enemy.

It became obvious presently that whoever he was he did not know the lie of the land very intimately. He had to halt at the edge of the ravine and stare under his hand to left and right in search of a place where he could cross.

"That's our old thief," said Narayan Singh in a tone of finality. "If we find a place on this side, and he on that, we shall meet the sooner."

He led off without a word, and it began to look as if we might meet our man in the bed of the ravine without the others being any wiser. But as soon as we got in motion half a dozen of them saw us and shouted to the rest, who whipped to a gallop and headed instantly all in one direction, where the top of a negotiable track lay hidden from our view beyond a bulge in the far wall of the ravine.

At that old Ali Baba halted until they had all passed him, and then suddenly began to ride full-pelt the other way. He still made no signal to us, but kept close to the edge of the ravine, and was obviously looking for another crossing higher up. So we followed suit, looking for a track on our side, and what with the irregular curve of the ravine and the speed at which all were moving we soon had several miles between us and the score or so who probably believed that Ali Baba was still with them.

We had long ceased to hear their shouts in the distance when we found a dangerous descent at last and forced our reluctant camels to risk their necks down it. It was more like a goat's ladder than a road, but it was evidently used at times by men, for Ali Baba came on its corresponding opening on his side, and took his chance too. It wasn't merely dangerous going; the heat of the ravine came up to meet us like fumes off the lid of Tophet, seeming to singe your eyelids, and the camels behaved as if they felt the same vertigo that we did.

A camel is a fool at down-hill work in any case; he sticks his supercilious nose in the air and paws about with his forefoot as if expecting somebody to come and put a cushion under it; and if there isn't anything to step on he just yells, and steps on nothing, and lets it go at that. When he lands by luck and ignorance on something solid, he doesn't know enough to stand there for a breath or two and get his balance, but yells again and goes careering on his way like a devil with the hornets after him. So we had some exciting intervals before we reached the bottom.

The heat down there was so intense that you could hardly see or think. It was one of those infernos that geologists pretend were sucked out by running water two or three hundred million years ago. Knowing no more geology than most prospectors and not believing half of that, I prefer to think with the Arabs and Narayan Singh that the devil made that place when he slid on his belly for the home plate after stealing two bases in Eden.

It was full of rocks and rugged islands, and several minutes passed before we caught sight of our old friend, who was hunting for us as nervously as we were for him. Even then, there was such a dancing heat-haze in the valley bottom that we had to look three times before we were sure it was he.

The old man knew us all right. He made his camel kneel, and waited for us in a hollow, over whose rim a man could not be seen standing from twenty paces off.

"*Il hamdul illah!*" he exclaimed as soon as we got near him. "It is true that Allah makes all things easy, though an old man's bones rebel against this kind of work. Ay-yee! But my loins ache! How fares Jimgrim?"

I told him most of what had happened, while he leaned against his camel's rump and munched dry dates, spitting out the stones between my feet; but I said nothing about that wrestling-bout with Mujrim.

"*Taib!*" he said at last. "If the she-wolf Jael is in Petra, we lambs have a chance left for our lives. What do you think? That old village-raider Ibrahim ben Ah, who waits where he was bidden wait, vows he will not stir another inch toward Abu Lissan — nay, not, for fifty Ali Higgs! The Avenger is on the move, and none knows which direction he is taking.

"Ibrahim is so afraid that he would not let me go without twenty men — an escort as he pretended, but a guard as a matter of fact — to prevent me from betraying him. Now they will be hunting for me in this *wadi,* and I must be gone before they discover me. Go you two to Ibrahim ben Ah instead of me, while I take the news to Jimgrim."

"Did Yussuf get through with his letter?" I asked.

"No. They caught him. He had it in mind to sell that letter of Jimgrim's. He swore there was a draft in it for fifty thousand pounds, and he offered to trade the lot for ten good camels.

"But they took the letter from him, being brigands, whereas he was but a sneak-thief; and when they opened it and found only a letter in English and a second envelope containing nothing, then they knew him for the liar I said he was."

"Did they read the letter?" I asked.

"No, none could read it. But he offered to read it for them; and, judging his life to be in danger, he told such a tale about Jimgrim and Jael and Ali Higg as set them all well by the ears.

"But the fool wasn't clever enough to stick to the truth. He told such a cock-and-bull story that they could make neither head nor tail of it, and when they asked me I laughed.

"So he denounced me, saying I was party to the tricking of Ali Higg, and what with one thing and another Ibrahim ben Ah was at his wits' end, knowing not what to believe. I thought he would kill the two of us, and was not pleased, for, *inshallah,* I can die a better death than in one halter with a dog like Yussuf.

"But Allah makes all things easy. Ibrahim decided at last to obey the order in the letter that I brought, seeing that the seal was on it, and to take us both along with him."

"I will stick that pig Yussuf when I find him!" swore Narayan Singh. "By the Prophet's body and my beard, he shall learn how a knife in the belly feels!"

"Too late to teach him that," laughed Ali Baba. "You would have to fight the vultures for his belly. His head lies one way, and his limbs the other.

"There came two men from different directions. Ibrahim knew both of them, and knew they would not dare lie to him. The one said that Ali Higg, with Jael and Ayisha and a score of men, was camped in a *fiumara* not far off. The other said that a certain Jimgrim — a person much resembling Ali Higg in general appearance, even to the bandage on his neck — was prowling to the south of us, also with twenty men.

"That was so contrary to Yussuf's story that, considering his gold earrings and the army pistol and the camel-trappings — nor forgetting the lie about the draft for fifty thousand pounds — it was decided on the spot that the earth would be well rid of him. He begged like a city thief, and chattered a lot more lies, but they tore him between camels and he talked no more."

"Killed him for his earrings, eh?" said I, not exactly relishing the prospect of a visit to that gang.

"Aye, but I have the earrings," the old fox answered, and showed them in the hollow of his hand.

Well, it doesn't take much to make you laugh on some occasions. Most of us have giggled in church or at a funeral. The thought of that old rascal being clever enough to steal such loot in the circumstances under the eyes of a hundred and forty bandits was a straw that tickled overstrung nerves past control.

Narayan Singh and I sat back on our camels' rumps and roared with laughter until the tears came. I believe old Ali Baba thought us mad; there was nothing remarkable about the incident to him, barring professional pride.

"What does this mean about Jimgrim and Ali Higg?" he asked when we left off laughing for lack of breath. "What does the sore Lion think he will accomplish by calling himself Jimgrim?"

But we could not enlighten him on that score, and he shook his head forebodingly.

"If this were my expedition, by Allah, I would call it off!" he exclaimed. "The thieves are too much disturbed for an honest man to make a profit. I like the thought of El-Kalil.

"However, those dogs of Ibrahim ben Ah's will catch me unless I hurry. Go ye to Ibrahim with them, and tell him any tale you please, so be you keep them off my trail until I reach our Jimgrim. Hark! I hear their voices."

HE WAS up and away with astonishing agility, riding at top speed up the ravine in search of a better track to escape by. I think if I had been alone I would have followed him, for it didn't look like wisdom or necessity to take tea just then with Ibrahim ben Ah. Our old fox had the news, and until Grim had a chance to pass judgment on it there was nothing much to be gained that I could see by running further risks.

But though I've often met men who pretended to no yellow streak, and have sometimes envied their ability to fool themselves, I'm disagreeably aware of a phase of fear that has got me into more tight places at different times than I care to recall. Perfectly aware of what was actuating me, I didn't care, nevertheless, to appear afraid before Narayan Singh.

"We'd better get a move on," I suggested.

He eyed me sharply once, and whatever his own thought process was, I'm pretty sure he was aware of mine.

"Why not?" he answered, laughing. "As our old king of thieves keeps on saying, 'Allah makes all things easy!' "

So we rode side by side down the *wadi* to meet Ibrahim's men, and they weren't pleased when they came on us and were assured that old Ali Baba had given them the slip. They swore outrageously. Their fear of returning without the old man provided an uncomfortable insight into the character of the other old man we would presently be forced to meet.

But swearing did not get them anywhere, and to have killed us on the spot, much though that would have suited their temper, might have got them into even worse trouble with their irascible commander. They were as tough a crowd of hard-faced cutthroats as ever praised Allah thrice a day, and they hadn't a camel between them that was half as good as either of our two.

So when they had failed by dint of threats to extort from us the slightest hint as to the direction old Ali Baba had taken they made up their minds to do the next best thing and ordered us to trade camels with them. But I think I've hinted once or twice that I like to make a profit on most transactions. I like to swing my strength into anything that comes along, take my chances with the next man, and get well paid for it.

There was nothing that appealed to me in the suggestion to trade two magnificent Syrian riding-camels for a couple of mangy baggage-beasts, especially since the good ones did not belong to me in any case. So I waxed exceeding wrathy. Long experience has taught me to be slow-spoken in anger, giving each abusive word full room and weight, in a voice like a good top-sergeant's to an awkward squad.

"In the name of the Prophet, on whom be peace," I thundered, "I can smite nine or ten such dogs as you! As many of you as are left afterward can return to Ibrahim ben Ah and tell him you met two friends of the Lion of Petra, who proved that jackals are no match for them!

"Come on!" said I. "Try to take the camels. Ye call yourselves the Lion's followers. Alley-dogs! Eaters of ullage! Try what the Lion's friends are like!"

A speech like that might not get you farther than the hospital, if you tried it in a railway round-house in the States, or even on a soap-box, say, on Fourteenth Street, New York, where the rag-tag and bob-tail of the universe foregather. But in the desert, where every contour of the landscape is a threat that must be taken seriously — and above all in a company whose leader's threats mean business — the voice of arrogance is likelier listened to than argument or whining.

Add to that that we were two big men, well armed — that my shaven head and sprouting beard suggested the *darwaish* and a form of religious sanctity — that we hadn't betrayed the slightest inclination to run away at any stage in the proceedings — and you can judge their predicament. They had their choice between calling the bluff or mending their manners; and the latter being easiest, they chose it.

On top of that I turned another trick, as old as politics. If you want at least the appearance of obedience, order a man to do what he wants to do. Knowing what they wanted, I didn't give them time to make demands, but announced mine high-handedly.

"Lead the way to Ibrahim ben Ah!" I commanded, and then added for the sake of sweet amenity, "Let us see what he has to tell us about changing camels!"

The situation was reversed forthwith. They began to be very friendly — almost obsequious. They addressed me as "your honor," and Narayan Singh as "prince," he being ostensibly a Pathan, a nation that does not run to princes, but likes flattery almost as much as fighting.

But they took the precaution of placing us in their midst before starting out of that infernal *wadi,* and there were moments while we made the difficult ascent when it was mighty comforting to know that Narayan Singh was on the camel next behind. He has eyes in the back of his head.

Once out of the ravine we lit out for the horizon at a clip too fast for conversation; and when they wanted to halt half-way and ask me questions I refused. Our destination was a low, long, flat-topped hill scattered with boulders that looked like warts on the back of a rhinoceros. The green of a few date palms at the right-hand end announced an oasis and the water that constitutes the key to all desert strategy. Whoever holds the wells commands that situation, and can oblige his adversary to f ight in that place first.

We slowed down as we drew near the encampment, and Narayan Singh poured out the vials of his military scorn, compared to which the scorn of one religious sect for another is as mere nursery stuff.

"Who could make a nation of such people!" he exclaimed. "Not a picket! Not an outpost! Not a sentry marking the camp limit! No wonder a tribe is strong one year and paying tribute the next. The very pickpockets of India know better than to sleep without mounting a guard."

But in spite of his contempt we were seen from a long way off, and although there was no guard turned out to receive us, the word had been passed to the commander several minutes before we reached the camp that two strangers were being brought in. He was the only one who had a tent — pretty obviously a stolen one, for it bore all the earmarks of the U. S. Near East Relief Commission. He did not come outside it to receive us. We could see him from a quarter of a mile away, seated on a pile of cushions, looking like an Old Testament king with his iron-gray beard and long robes.

As soon as we came within range of his eyes through the open tent-front our escort tried to stage what the armies call "eye-wash," but failed to get away with it. They closed in on us, seeking to give the impression that we were prisoners. However, eye-wash, which is after all but the name of a sub-species of bluff, was all that Narayan Singh and I had to depend on; so we halted promptly, and used our tongues and camel-sticks.

"Fathers of a bad smell!" I roared at them. "Shall we approach Ibrahim ben Ah stinking like unwashed village-dogs? Keep clear of us! Keep behind!"

And because of the likelihood of retribution if they should be seen handling us roughly, in the possible event of our finding favor, they obeyed and hauled off.

So we rode alone in advance, looking more like officers of a platoon than prisoners. The bivouac was made at the foot of the northern slope of the hill, with the camels lying in irregular lines all about a row of three deep wells, whose masonry gleamed in the fierce sun-light between thrifty date-palms.

Most of the men were sprawling here and there on mats. Some had made shelters of their prayer-mats propped on short sticks, and there was one long shed that would hold thirty or forty men made by spreading mats on poles across the heaped-up camel-loads. They had plenty of baggage with them — mainly stuff to eat — but the loads were all intact and ready to be moved at a moment's notice.

Whether for sake of example, or by way of humor, or as a hint to strangers, or as a practical, artistic means of establishing the limit of the bivouac, they had stuck Yussuf's head on a spear-point, and the ghastly, sightless thing leered at us as we rode by. There was no sign of the other remnants of him.

I never got over feeling squeamish about that kind of thing, and the feeling of more or less confidence that I had raised in myself by brow-beating the escort petered out pretty badly. Narayan Singh didn't appear to mind the gruesome spectacle, but feelings in concrete instances like that are individual, and his indifference failed to impart itself to me. His own may have been assumed for all I know.

The escort shouted to us to dismount and approach Ibrahim ben Ah respectfully on foot — which would have placed us in the attitude of inferiors. It is none of my intention to challenge Holy Writ, and the meek may inherit the earth with no impediment from me, but I main-tain there are occasions when meekness is dangerous weakness.

Besides, I don't like abject salutations when addressed to me. Mis-trusting, as I invariably do, any man who shows me too much out-ward respect, it's no less than reasonable to reverse that and hold my chin as high as I expect the other fellow to. Anyway I've always done it, and I did so then.

We rode straight up to Ibrahim ben Ah's tent and let our camels kneel before dismounting. Then in our own good time, Narayan Singh taking his cue from me out of the corner of his eye, we gave the desert greeting that is solemn, stately, dignified, raising our hands to our foreheads as we bowed.

"Salamun alaik!" said I.

"Wa alaik issalam!" answered Ibrahim ben Ah.

Greeting and answer both meant "Peace!" So thus far all was well.

CHAPTER VII

"Akbar Ali Higg!"

THE last time we set eyes on Ibrahim ben Ah was in the desert on the way to Petra, on the occasion of our capturing Jael, when he strode into our midst at midnight to receive orders from Grim, whom he supposed in the darkness to be Ali Higg, and strode away again without comment.

It was likely he knew neither of us by sight, for he can't have had more than a sidewise glimpse of either of us in the always tricky moonlight; but I would have known him in any circumstances, for he was one of those rare individuals who leave their impress ineradicably on your mind, unlike Grim, who seems to have the useful gift of fading, so that every time you see him after an interval you remark something unexpected about him that seems new.

You can't forget what Grim has done, nor how he did it, although it's difficult to describe him because his features are not easy to recall. You could very easily forget what Ibrahim ben Ah had done, and his methods were too crude and cruel to possess the slightest novelty; but you couldn't forget his face and general appearance if you tried for twenty years.

He was a handsome old fellow, with the venerable aspect rather spoiled by the breadth of his nose and the cold acquisitiveness of keen blue eyes. You expected them to be brown, and it was rather a shock when you saw they weren't.

Most men look smaller when seated, especially if the seat is a mat or a pile of cushions, but not so he. The position merely increased his dignity.

He wore quite a lot of jewelry, including several diamond rings that called attention to the great size of his shapely hands, which were wrinkled and brown, but strong as iron. Most of his garments, except the striped outer cloak, were of silk, but, unlike most of his men, who wore plundered boots of every conceivable pattern, his bare, brown feet were shod only with open sandals.

He had the usual allowance of two bandoleers, a British service rifle, a revolver and two knives in sight; and they were probably only a suggestion of the armory he kept hidden from view in the ample folds of his cloak. When he moved there was a suggestive clink of hardware.

On the whole, I am inclined to think his main secret of command was hypnotic; he was so used to the receipt and execution of ruthless orders, and so bent on being obeyed that authority exuded from him like an aura. I made up my mind right away that to humor him would only tickle his vanity.

His men were within easy hail, and ten or twelve ruffians were standing almost within earshot; but inside the tent there were two of us to one of him, and if there was going to be any high-handed business I had a notion who would be first to regret it. Instead of waiting for him to speak first and standing respectfully in front of him, as ninety-nine Indians out of any hundred would have done, I squatted down on the floor-mat, motioned to Narayan Singh to do the same, and opened on him with an awkward question.

"What is this tale we hear?" I demanded. "Ali Higg sends us to find Ali Baba. Ali Baba tells us that you are afraid to advance on Abu Lissan. What does it mean?"

He was dumbfounded. There were probably not more than three people in the world who had dared to question him like that for several years past.

"Where is Ali Baba, and who are you that ask such a question?" he demanded after a long pause.

"Ali Baba," said I, "is obeying orders, conveyed from the Lion himself by me to him. He has gone back to tell the Lion all that he has seen and heard. As to who I am — *Mashallah!* Are the Lion's envoys called in question?"

"You are a stranger to me," he retorted.

"Not so," said I. "I was with the Lion on the night when he ordered you to that oasis on the way to El-Maan. I am the *hakim* who healed his boils. This other is my servant. I am a *darwaish* from Lahore, well versed in such matters as pertain to the offsetting of greater force by strategy and cunning. Therefore I am now employed by Ali Higg to aid him in confounding the Avenger."

"Cunning?" he said, with the suggestion of a wry smile. "You look more like a bold man than a cunning one. Let us hope you are the father of deceit, for as surely as this right hand strikes my left, not the Prophet himself could have prevailed in his day against such numbers as we have against us!"

He suited action to the word by bringing down his right fist into his left palm with a loud clap.

As I have said several times, I am no strategist. That trick would have got by me. But Narayan Singh was too alert for him, and before the nearest men could come running in answer to the signal Ibrahim ben Ah's cold old eyes were staring disconcertedly straight down the muzzle of a Webley revolver.

All the odds were dreadfully against us except one, but that lone one outweighed the rest. In common with the normal run of men old Ibrahim ben Ah was unprepared to die, and something in his inner consciousness convinced him — accurately as it happened — that Narayan Singh would pull the trigger, and not miss, unless he sent the men away as swiftly as he had summoned them.

I was afraid for a second that he was going to be too late, in which case I suppose this story would never have been told, although Ibrahim ben Ah and half a dozen others would certainly have preceded us to hammer at the gates of Kingdom Come. The old rascal was so surprised that words stuck in his throat, and I drew my own repeating pistol in readiness to make a last stand alongside Narayan Singh. But Ibrahim barked out an order in the nick of time, and almost at the tent-door the men halted, and turned away without having seen what was happening because the Sikh's broad back was turned toward them.

Ibrahim ben Ah screwed up a smile that showed the gold caps on his eye-teeth when the men were once more out of ear-shot and Narayan Singh lowered the revolver.

"Ye act like men who are afraid!" he sneered. "Ye fear without cause. By Allah, I am a man who is well served, and if my men mistake a chance noise for a summons, that is no reason why honest men should tremble for their lives." But if any one was trembling it was he, and not with fear but anger almost too intense to be suppressed. Having won the upper hand of him mainly through Narayan Singh's presence of mind, it was up to us to hold it, and about as certain as anything well could be that the old man would reverse the situation at the first chance.

"I asked a question that you haven't answered yet," said I. "By the Prophet's feet, this is a fine reception for the Lion's messengers! A strange tale we shall have to tell him!"

"Aye!" he croaked, moving his Adam's apple several times in rapid succession as he choked down his rising passion. "A very strange tale, on top of stranger happenings; I would like to see how Ali Higg with twenty men can make me move with a hundred, four and forty!

"First it was toward the British border I was sent, to raid El-Maan, which was feasible; there is loot there for the taking. Then I was told to cool my heels in that oasis. Now it is to march on Abu Lissan, where we have no chance at all, and I am sick of the changing orders from day to day.

"By Allah, who am I to be ordered about like a bought slave? And who in the name of the Prophet is Ali Higg that he should play fast and loose with me? I will not march on Abu Lissan, and that is all about it!"

I laughed. I couldn't think of anything to say for the moment. If Ali Higg's main force was going to mutiny, I didn't see that Grim had much chance left of checkmating the Avenger and restoring a kind of order on the countryside. My main trouble is that I think too slowly to be of much use in a crisis of that kind; but Narayan Singh stepped nobly into the breach.

"By Allah's Prophet and my teeth!" he boomed out. "Say thy prayers, Ibrahim! These men who obey thee at a hand-clap shall choose between thee and a woman presently!"

"Jael has returned to Petra," he answered rather smugly.

Narayan Singh had Ayisha in mind, not Jael; but here was a new note in the discord. Evidently Jael had got word to Ibrahim by one of those three messengers who brought news to Ayisha in the night; and Ibrahim had drawn his own conclusions.

I SAW clearly now the strength of Grim's contention in refusing to divulge his plans. If he had outlined any definite course for us to follow I would have felt bound by it; whereas I was free to use my own judgment as it was.

If Ibrahim ben Ah had determined, as seemed possible, to desert with all his force to the Avenger rather than run the risk of defeat, we stood confronted with a fine kettle of fish. The Avenger would be free, for one thing, to establish himself as paramount chief of all that district; success would breed success; next he might capture El-Kerak — perhaps Es-Salt as well — and raid like a whirlwind into Palestine with thousands of loot-hungry malcontents.

From my own personal standpoint I wouldn't have worried much if the Avenger should accomplish all those things, for sooner or later he would be brought to bay and smashed by the British army. It didn't seem to me that the price of U. S. Government securities would be affected.

But I was set like any decent member of a team on seeing Grim win out. You can't like a man and not do your darnedest to help him win the game, even if it isn't your game exactly. And my game, too, it was, to the extent that Narayan Singh's life and mine were teetering in the balance.

You can't explain thought processes, or at any rate I can't. Something takes place inside your tympanum, and you act or speak. If the gray stuff functions neatly, you say or do the right thing; then you're a wise one. If it doesn't, the temporary lessees of other sorts of cerebellums describe you afterward as a fool or a poor fish, while some one cashes in on the insurance and the undertaker makes another entry in his ledger.

So don't put me down as a psychologist, for I'm only guessing when I say that keenness on the job has a lot to do with inspiration. To state a case with proper caution, "I've observed" that when you're really keen to help another man, you're more likely to do the right thing than the wrong one, even in the dark.

"Have you heard about Jimgrim?" I asked him, and the question went straight as a bullet into the very center of his perplexity.

So I'm a wise one, even though I did shoot at a venture.

"Heard of him? May Allah change his face!" he snarled. "Aye, I have heard of him. What do you know of him? What is he doing, prowling the desert with twenty men, and sending me messages? They say he resembles Ali Higg, even to the wrappings on his neck. What is his purpose?"

"Tell me what message he sent you, and perhaps I can answer," said I.

"He sent word to me at dawn today to run no risks, but to wait in this place until he shall speak with the Avenger. What does that mean?"

It obviously meant that the Lion of Petra, pretending to be Grim — even as Grim was pretending to be the Lion of Petra — was venturing on the risky course of trading on Grim's reputation. How he could hope to escape being recognized by the Avenger, whose face he boasted of having spoiled, was past imagining; but it was easy to understand why he should want to keep Ibrahim ben Ah inactive until he should have a chance to try the trick.

"What does his impudence mean?" Ibrahim repeated.

But I am too old a bird to be caught airing my knowledge at the first request. Information, like hard cash, is for use, not squandering.

"Why didn't you catch him and find out?" I asked.

"Wallahi! If I could have caught him I would have flayed the fool alive! I sent twoscore men after him, but he was gone. Does the Lion know about him?" he asked with sudden suspicion. "Is Ali Higg employing him to make terms with the Avenger?"

But I hedged again. If I could keep Ibrahim ben Ah from deserting to the other side by stimulating doubt, that looked like good business.

"I am in the Lion's confidence," said I. "Tell me what you know of Jimgrim; then — dates in exchange for rice, camels for horses, sheep for wheat — if the trade looks good I will tell what I know in return."

"Jimgrim," he said slowly, speaking through his teeth as a man does when he mentions sacrilege or anything else that he detests, "is an Amiricani, an infidel, who has been to Mecca, to my knowledge, in disguise. He was useful to Feisul and Lawrence in the great war, when we Arabs defeated the Turks, and the Allies took the credit and the plunder. He is a bold man, with the cunning of a hundred. And he once saved a day for Saoud the Avenger by getting camels for him when the Turks had captured most of the Avenger's beasts."

"So if Jimgrim should get to the Avenger's ear he might listen on the score of friendship?" I suggested.

"Wallahi! That might be. The point is, what will Jimgrim say to the Avenger?"

I nodded; but I knew that wasn't the point. If there was one dead certainty on earth, it was that the Lion of Petra, whether or not disguised as Grim, would never dare trespass into the Avenger's camp, for fear of recognition and the inevitably gruesome death that would certainly follow. An Arab doesn't dub himself "Avenger" and then forgive the mortal enemy detected in the act of tricking him. However, my job seemed to be to keep Ibrahim on tenterhooks.

"Jimgrim is in league with the Lion," I said, quite truthfully.

Following that, I drew hard on imagination.

"Jimgrim's plan," I continued, "is to take camels away from the Avenger for a change. There are men in the Avenger's camp who will desert at Jimgrim's bidding, driving off the camels with them."

And, having known a little frankness on occasion to leaven a prodigious lot of lies, I added —

"The Lion suspects you of intending treachery."

"Allah!" he exclaimed, trying to cover up alarm with a display of indignation.

"By Allah, yes!" said I. "And if Jimgrim should return from Abu Lissan with a couple of hundred of the Avenger's best men, it would fare badly with any traitor in this camp."

At the word traitor the irascible old bandit made a motion as if to draw one of his weapons. But he thought better of it. Narayan Singh's revolver was too obviously pointed straight, and my own pistol was equally in evidence.

The deuce of it was that, though we held him helpless for the moment, the situation was going to be reversed the moment we should try to escape. We could prevent his men from coming to his assistance easily enough, by threatening to shoot him unless he ordered them away again; but either we had got to sit there watching him until we all starved, or until the god of all improbabilities should produce Grim on the scene, or else I had got to take a one-in-a-hundred-thousand chance.

I took a silver five-piaster piece from the purse in the fold of my waist-cloth, and spun it in the air. It fell on the mat tails uppermost. The long chance had it.

"Will you sit here," I said to Narayan Singh, "and keep the old bird company, while I take a turn outside."

Ibrahim ben Ah did not understand a word of that, but he dropped his jaw at hearing me speak English. But surprise gave place to baffled anger as the Sikh answered me in Arabic.

"Surely. I will keep his honor company. Moreover, I speak for his honor Ibrahim, who will sit quietly, as becomes a courteous host, to wait for your return — seeing he is averse to having three holes shot through him with this revolver!" he added meaningly.

Ibrahim ben Ah said never a word. I don't see what there was he could have said. Barring unforseen contingencies, we had him corralled for the moment. I got up and left the tent with the notion first of all of finding out just how far Ibrahim's intention of betraying Ali Higg had taken root among the men.

Seeing one come out leisurely where two had entered, the men who happened to be watching drew no conclusions that troubled them. They lay under their improvised shelters eying me with lazy interest, more curious than suspicious.

There wasn't any of that sullen look about them that most Eastern, and all African, peoples wear when they think of betraying their salt. It was a long shot — the longest I ever risked — but I made up my mind to behave as if I knew they were loyal to the last man to the Lion their master.

Don't forget: I was dressed and shaven for the part of a *darwaish*—

the politico-religious fanatic, who is privileged more or less to air his opinions on any subject, and whose person is theoretically sacred from assault. No theories are fool-proof, and no *darwaish* should strain his immunity too far, but he has privileges that are more likely to be respected by the ignorant than by their leaders.

There was nothing outrageous, or even surprising, in my assumption of an air of superior wisdom and arrogance. Besides, coming straight out of Ibrahim's tent, it was presumable that I had his authority for whatever I might say or do. They would reason that he would have ordered me to be beaten or murdered otherwise.

THERE was a big pile of flour-bags in the middle of the bivouac that made a first-class pulpit. I mounted it with as much of an air of frenzy as a man of my temperament can assume without looking foolish, and stood glaring about me until curiosity brought most of them to their feet.

"*Allaho Akbar!*" I roared then at the top of my lungs; and that being a subject on which all Moslems are unanimous, they shouted back at me that God was very great indeed.

The phrase being their favorite war-cry, as well as a statement of doctrine, they began to gather around me. I had my rifle in my right hand, and shook it violently by way of further stimulating curiosity, and in less than two minutes pretty nearly every member of the force was elbowing for standing room. You couldn't have gathered a crowd more easily in New York City.

When you're broke it's no use figuring on the pile you should have; then's the time to use nickels for all they're worth. And in a desperate situation it isn't any good worrying about what you don't know; the thing is to act on what you do know. Then if circumstances get the upper hand in spite of energy and courage, nobody can blame you. At least, they'll blame you, but they haven't any right to, which is different.

I knew one or two things for a fact. One was that Grim has genius, that he stands by his friends, and that he was keener than anybody on finding a solution of the general mess. Another certainty was that Ali Baba had gone to tell him the facts of the situation.

It wasn't going to help me or anybody else to take into the reckoning just then the possibility of Ali Baba failing to find Grim. That was up to Providence and Ali Baba.

A third indisputable fact was that Grim had stated his intention of putting Ayisha in command of these hundred and forty men. That made three things that I knew, which the men in front of me did not. It didn't look easy to build a compelling argument out of them, but I could try.

And a fourth fact — that they imagined Grim was Ali Higg, and Ali Higg was Grim, but that I knew the truth of the matter — provided an element of confusion, which any professional spell-binder could easily turn to advantage. Not being a trained orator gave me no right to lie down on the job, and I waded in. *"Allaho Akbar!"* I roared again.

I can bellow like a mad bull on suitable occasion.

"Allaho Akbar!" they answered.

We were getting on finely. A common platform was established. It was as if a soap-box orator in Union Square had started his speech by asserting that the Stars and Stripes is a first-class flag; whoever didn't think so in the audience would have to pretend to agree for his hat's sake. There was no fear of opposition now for a minute or two. "Ye followers of the Lion of Petra," I thundered out, "heroes of the desert — faithful followers of the true Prophet, on whom be peace — I bring word to you from Ali Higg, your leader."

"Akbar!" they began to shout.

So I had guessed right. It was only their commander who was disaffected.

I held up the rifle again for silence, and kept them waiting, having often noticed that the pauses are the best part of a speech.

"Ali Higg the terrible, the Lord of the Limits of the Desert and the Waters, has declared against Saoud in the name of Allah. Saoud, who dares to call himself Avenger, shall lie low!"

"Akbar! Akbar Ali Higg!" they shouted; for shouting costs nothing in any language, and commits nobody as long as reporters are not present.

"This fellow who calls himself Avenger has eight hundred men," I went on. "But what are numbers? Had the Prophet numbers when he marched against his enemies? Allah makes all things easy!"

"Allaho Akbar!" they agreed. "This Avenger fellow is a jackal, but he of Petra is a Lion. And like a lion he has taken to the desert, where cunning and craft win the day against numbers, even as the wind can blow the sand."

I was far from being certain of that simile; but my audience were not pedagogs. They were men who wanted to listen to optimism, and didn't care whether sand or wind resembled a lion's cunning, or otherwise.

"And does a lion hunt in company?" I demanded, glaring about me as if I had propounded a problem such as only a sage could answer. "Nay! He hunts alone! He stalks. He lies in wait. He strikes at the unexpected moment. And who can stand against him? He is terrible in his wrath, and his enemies are confused, not knowing the path he took nor the direction of his coming. Woe then, to the Lion's enemies!"

That part of the speech had such a good effect on them that I paused again to let the emotion work; and, glaring this and that way with a rolling eye, as I have seen the professionals behave, I got a chance to observe Ibrahim ben Ah's tent. The old man was still sitting in there, cursing steadily, I should say, by the way his beard moved; and Narayan Singh was so well placed that you couldn't possibly tell from outside the tent that he held a cocked revolver in his hand. The two seemed to be deep in conversation.

"But how about the Lion's friends?" I roared as soon as there was perfect silence. "Does he desert them? Never! Does he leave them to their own resources? No! Does he leave them at the mercy of an old man, whose days are numbered, whose marrowless bones might quake at the thought of facing the Avenger? Do ye think that the Lion would do such a thing?"

I paused once more, and as they did not know what was coming they held their breath.

"What think ye of the Lion's wife?"

"Jael! Jael!" they began to shout, and I didn't contradict them.

I didn't dare mention Ayisha yet, because the news of her divorce might possibly have reached them. The main point was to establish the thought in their minds that Ali Higg was going to send a woman deputy to override, and perhaps replace altogether, old Ibrahim ben Ah.

"The Lion's wife knows all his plans," I went on. "She keeps his secrets. She understands the craft with which he hunts. She has courage, and guile, and ability. Are ye afraid to follow a woman? Has a woman never led you to victory?"

They made no secret of the fact that they preferred a woman. Possibly even Jael's discipline was less fierce than Ibrahim ben Ah's or Ali Higg's.

"Good! We will follow his wife!" they shouted.

"He has more than one wife," I countered then. "What does it matter to you which wife he sends?"

They said it made no difference. I think they rather hoped a junior wife would come, whose hand would fall less heavily than Jael's on offenders. They were just as feckless in the hour of uncertainty as any other crowd of men — the usual human mixture of emotions, fierce and sheep-like alternately — accustomed to be led, and consequently afraid of nothing so much as to be left to their own resources.

Can you think of one crowd of rebels since history was written that in a climax wasn't eager for a change of captains? They were still full of confidence in Ali Higg, because he had always held himself as much as possible aloof from them. He was a sort of mystery, who led them once in a while in person on some whirlwind foray, and who imposed his drastic punishments more often than not by deputy. So Ibrahim ben Ah, the deputy, was a weariness to the flesh, while Ali Higg remained a hero in their imaginations.

I dare say that in that minute I could have led a mutiny against Ibrahim ben Ah. It would only have called for a little mouthing of religious platitudes — quotations from the Koran — any of the pabulum with which all agitators fool the crowd into believing it has justice on its side; for you can't do much, even with a crowd of pirates, unless you make them think the issue is a moral one.

But — setting aside the fact that mutinous troops are useless to anybody; and Grim, as far as I understood the situation, wanted a force in being to maneuver against the Avenger — there is something in my make-up that rebels against that sort of thing. It strikes me as playing off-side, and I don't enjoy to win my point, earn money, or resolve a difficulty that way.

To trick an opponent is one thing. To take him by surprise, catch him napping, cause him to deceive himself, and, if he is a man of violence, feed him his own medicine, is all in the game, as I see it. But to defeat even a bandit by deliberately stirring mutiny among his men seems to me to put you in the class with propagandists in other people's countries; it's no white man's business.

So I didn't say one word further about Ibrahim ben Ah. For all I cared, and if they chose to submit to it, he might lead them to the devil once that hand was played; that was their affair, and his. Old Ibrahim got much the worst of the transaction; but I'd enjoy to meet him tomorrow and talk the matter over.

That's one of the reasons why Grim and I get on so well together in spite of his uncommunicativeness; I have never known him to play with cards under the table. He plays good poker. He can bluff like a Down-East Yankee, drawing nothing to a pair of jacks and winning by the glitter in his eye. But he plays a white man's game; and I've never known him spiteful.

However, there I was on a pile of flour-bags in the baking sun, wondering what to say next. As I have explained, the bivouac rested in the curve near one end of a boulder-strewn hill. You couldn't see around the corner, but in front and to the left was empty desert, smirched here and there with sand-clouds driven by the scorching wind.

The only men on watch whom I could see were half a dozen posted on the lower end of the spur that cut off the right-hand view, although there may have been one or two others hidden among the boulders on the top of the hill behind me.

For lack of any better entertainment I was about to tell them of the plunder there might be in Abu Lissan, that being a subject that would have amused them without committing me in any way, when I detected symptoms of excitement among the watchers on the spur of the hill to my right. That could only possibly mean that somebody was coming.

The crowd was facing me. I waved my rifle in the direction of the lookout, and they all faced about to see. That gave me time to think, and I thought first of Narayan Singh.

If any one except Grim were coming, the Sikh and I were as good as dead men; for visitors would certainly be taken straight to Ibrahim ben Ah's tent, and you could trust that old opportunist to turn the tables on us promptly at the first chance. We would have to shoot in self-defense, and it would be all over in a minute.

So it wasn't the least use speculating on that contingency. The only possible chance of safety lay in the arrival of Grim, and in his being mistaken for Ali Higg. I must bet on that; and being so constituted that I habitually use the last shot as determinedly as the first one, I went the limit.

"Aha!" I roared. "The Lion of Petra comes! To your camels! I go to tell Ibrahim ben Ah!"

AT THE first suggestion of anything doing the Bedouin thinks of his camel in any case. Each man rushed away to where his beast lay hobbled. They tie a rope around his folded foreleg after the camel has been made to kneel, and that prevents his getting up until the rope is loosed again.

I jumped off the pile of bags and strode, as slowly as I could contrive in the state of excitement I was in, toward Ibrahim ben Ah's tent, where Narayan Singh still sat motionless with his back toward me.

The lookout on the spur began shouting before I was half-way to the tent. I couldn't hear the words, but the men nearest to them did, and passed the news along. Instantly the bivouac was in an uproar, and camels began rising to their feet in twos and threes and dozens as the hobbles were untied.

"*Akbar Ali Higg!*" they roared in greeting.

So Grim was coming!

But as I reached the tent, old Ibrahim ben Ah seemed to me to be wearing a rather too confident smile for a man in his predicament. I think he counted on a dozen or more men running to the tent with news, in which case we should be overwhelmed. He probably argued that, in view of Ali Higg's arrival, we would hesitate to shoot first.

"Between promise and fulfillment a man may marry off his ugly daughter," is a proverb with which every Arab in extremity consoles himself; and I knew as well as he did that between the moment of Grim's turning the corner of the hill and his reaching the tent a hundred things might happen.

If we should be killed in the interval, whether we were the Lion's friends or not, and whether or not he set high value on us, as dead men we should never be able to explain the incident or deny any made-up yarn of Ibrahim's.

So I enlightened him on one point, to begin with. I stood in the tent opening with my pistol leveled straight at him.

"What is written is written," I said, "and none knoweth any outcome before it cometh to pass. But I know this pistol is a good one, and is loaded. If it is written that blood shall flow now, of us three you die first, friend Ibrahim ben Ah!"

He decided to sit still, luckily for him. But it was an uncomfortable minute. There is nothing pleasant about holding a pistol at an old man's head, or in the possible necessity to shoot him, for that matter.

But luckily for us Grim was at the top of his form that morning. He had taken his time about following us across the desert, reserving all his speed for the last lap, when speed and nothing else could count.

There wasn't a chance in a million of his being able to keep up the pretense of being Ali Higg if he lingered among the men, or once came within eye-shot of Ibrahim. He had to pull off one swift, convincing bluff, or else we were all in the discard together.

I got behind Ibrahim ben Ah, so as to see what was going on without losing the upper hand of him. I touched the back of his head with the muzzle of my pistol, and watched as if Babe Ruth were making a home run.

Suddenly Grim swooped around the corner at full gallop, followed by Ali Baba and his sixteen rascals with Ayisha in their midst, and I nodded to Narayan Singh to get to his feet as the bandits shook their rifles in the air and thundered out their greeting —

"Akbar Ali Higg!"

CHAPTER VIII

"Have you heard of Jimgrim?"

GRIM had left no more to chance than was necessary. He had even wrapped his neck with bandages to heighten his resemblance to the Lion; and the lower half of his face being covered for protection against the wind, it was easy enough to mistake his identity.

Another point in his favor was the real Ali Higg's notorious aloofness. It was in keeping with the part that he should halt a hundred yards beyond the limit of the bivouac and wait in solitary grandeur while his men came on to do his bidding.

Nor was it anything remarkable that those accompanying him should be strangers to Ibrahim's command, for unless such a robber chief as Ali Higg can keep on adding fresh parties of marauders to his string he is pretty surely doomed to collapse.

Evidently Grim had left no detail of his plan unexplained this time; and he had the advantage of Ali Baba's familiarity with the lay of things. Our seventeen rascals with Ayisha in their midst came on at top speed, straight for the tent, where it might be expected that Narayan Singh and I would be, since we were nowhere else in evidence.

Midway, Ayisha whirled aside to confront and harangue the lined-up camel-men; and she showed the same sort of form that she did at El-Maan railway station when we first saw her in action. Under the very eyes of Ali Higg himself they could hardly do other than hear her respectfully; but you don't have to be a savage to get all worked up when a pretty young woman with a rifle in her hand screams warlike exhortations at you from a blooded camel. She thrilled me; and I had something else to think about.

It didn't look good to me to leave old Ibrahim ben Ah to stew in his resentment, and perhaps to spoil Ayisha's game at a critical moment. Having no notion what the game might be, still it was hardly a stroke of genius to suppose that she would play it more easily without that handicap. On the other hand, it looked no better to submit him to indignity before his men. If they once got the notion in their heads that Ibrahim ben Ah was in disgrace, they would be all the more likely to try to take advantage of Ayisha, because, as the Turks are so fond of saying, "a fish begins stinking from the head." The suggestion that a commander can be deposed in the field spreads insubordination in the rank and file.

I had made up my mind what to do, whether Grim should approve or not, before Ali Baba and his sixteen reached the tent and halted in a cloud of dust. Our two camels were kneeling twenty feet away; and Ibrahim ben Ah's magnificent beast, all hung with worsted ornaments and blue beads, was standing at a picket close by.

"It is time for you two to come!" called Ali Baba with a note of almost desperate excitement in his raven voice.

"Nay, three of us!" I shouted back. "Send two men in here swiftly. Let a third bring the commander's camel."

There was one thing about those thieves of ours; they were used to teamwork, and. in any kind of crisis they were as swift as lightning. Nobody stopped to argue. I tapped the muzzle of my pistol on Ibrahim's shoulder.

"Now," said I, "alive or dead, you're coming with us to Ali Higg yonder. If you want to save your face before your men, act dignified. We're either a guard of honor or a prisoner's escort, whichever you prefer. You may keep your weapons for the present, but I'll take them all away from you in front of your men and make you walk to Ali Higg if you try to start any kind of trouble. Get up!"

He didn't try anything. The old man liked his dignity too well. He rose to his feet without a word. Mujrim and Mahommed closed in on either side of him, and led him to his camel.

The gang reformed platoon. Our old fox Ali Baba brought his camel alongside Ibrahim's, and led off, followed by Narayan Singh and me with our pistols ready but not too openly displayed. Behind us rode the sixteen, eight abreast. Not even Xerxes, King of Persia, ever rode from his tent with greater apparent honor, and I gravely doubt whether even Ayisha, all eyes though she was for everything and all alert for information, suspected until we were gone that Ibrahim ben Ah had been made prisoner.

We rode out of the bivouac at a walk, as any general with his staff might go to attend a conference. And when we came within a hundred yards of Grim he wheeled and rode away ahead of us, answering the roars of the Bedouins with a curt wave of the hand. A minute later he swung at a gallop around the corner of the hill, and we were hard put to it to overtake him.

But he wouldn't let me draw abreast to compare notes yet. Grim is one of those fellows who, if he had the part of Othello to act, would blacken his skin all over. We were still visible to the lookout on the spur, and perhaps to others on the hill-top. He signed to me to keep my distance, for it seemed that Ali Higg had a reputation for preferring to ride all by himself in advance of his men.

So I had to bide my time until we reached that same deep *wadi* in which Narayan Singh and I had talked with Ali Baba, and I didn't spend it envying Ayisha, with the job on her hands of maneuvering a hundred and forty cutthroats in accordance with some secret plan; though I dare say she asked nothing better, if only because she was usurping Jael's prerogative.

Our baggage beasts were kneeling in a fine hiding-place between boulders, not far from where we had come on Ali Baba, and there Grim halted at last for a talk, and we all gathered around him in the shadow of an overhanging rock.

IBRAHIM BEN AH opened on him without preliminary, and with no more courtesy than the Prophet Elijah, for instance, used to show toward sinful Israelitish kings.

"Who are you, who pose as the Lion of Petra?" he demanded angrily of Jimgrim.

"Does it matter?" Grim answered smiling.

"Malaish!" he retorted. "No, no matter. A dog comes to a dog's end! Death and a dung-hill — *khallas!* [finish!]"

"Isn't it a little soon to talk of dogs and dung-hills?" Grim answered pleasantly. "One friend is better than a hundred enemies."

At that there came into Ibrahim ben Ah's eyes a look of calculating, cold cupidity. When men of the desert kidnap important people, they kill them or hold them to ransom; that is the accepted procedure. They certainly don't offer to make friends with them unless their own position is too desperate for ordinary measures. And desperate folk must accept exacting terms. The very bristles of the old man's beard seemed to move as his temper changed, and he eyed Grim with a rising insolence.

"What does such a man as you imagine he can offer me?" he demanded:

Grim laughed good-temperedly.

"Perhaps only a choice of evils. But a choice is something. I might send you back to Petra for Jael to laugh at."

The savage old commander's mood changed rapidly once more.

"By Allah," he snarled, "I will make no bargains with a tent sneak-thief! Do thy worst, son of a dog!"

"You're going to have no chance to make a bargain," Grim answered. "There's an offer going to be made to you. You may accept it and smile, or reject it and take the consequences. None of us is going to be inconvenienced in either case."

Ibrahim ben Ah became bewildered. He sat down cross-legged on the sand, with a gesture implying that the future lay in Allah's lap. If he had been deprived of his weapons and jewels, perhaps he might have thought he understood; but there gleamed the diamonds on his fingers; there were his rifle — pistols — knives; and instead of scowling, talking about ransom or threatening torture his captor smiled at him good-humoredly and talked conundrums.

"Inshallah, we shall see," he said simply.

So Grim sat down too and folded his arms, with his back to the sunlight, in position to read the old man's face. You can glean more information from a man's passing expressions than from anything he says, in most instances, provided you own the proper eyes for the business.

"Have you heard of Jimgrim?" Grim asked him; and Ibrahim's eyes opened wider by a fraction of an inch.

"I have ears. Surely I have heard of him. An infidel, who went to Mecca in defiance of the Moslem law. An unbelieving dog, who should be shown no quarter."

"I am Jimgrim," Grim assured him pleasantly.

"I knew it!" answered our venerable captive; and his eyes closed again ever so slightly, so that I don't think he had even guessed the fact until that minute. "I dare say you know all about me?"

Ibrahim screwed up his face, something after the fashion of a Christian missionary who is asked to give his opinion of the active agent of a rival denomination.

"Most men in this land have heard of you. You have a name for being clever."

"And a liar?"

"No, I have not heard that said of you."

"Do you remember what I was doing in the great war?"

"Surely. I heard of you. You worked for Feisul."

"Didn't you work for him too?" demanded Grim.

"By Allah, that I did! So did we all. Feisul is the rightful king of all this land. A true descendant of the Prophet. A son of the king of Mecca. A God-fearing man, on whom be peace! Would I might lead a squadron behind Feisul again!"

"Then in that we are agreed," said Grim. "Feisul is the rightful king of all this land."

"Yes — if it is my last word on earth!"

"I worked for Feisul in the war. I'm working for him now," said Grim.

"Then why do you make a prisoner of me, a friend of his?"

"My old friend Ali Baba told me that you contemplated going over to Saoud the Avenger with most of Ali Higg's men," Grim replied evasively.

"I never told him that!"

"Possibly. But a fox can guess which way a rooster means to run."

"Well, he guessed shrewdly," Ibrahim answered after a moment's pause.

He seemed to be making up his mind that nothing could be gained by not humoring his interrogator. "I am sick of Ali Higg, the Lion of Petra. The Avenger has eight hundred men already; a hundred and forty more would make him a power in the land."

"And a general of you, eh? But Saoud the Avenger is out for himself, not for Feisul."

"So is Ali Higg out for himself and not for Feisul. And Feisul is a puppet ruler in Damascus, waiting to be turned out by the French and sent begging."

"But you are for Feisul," said Grim.

"Surely. But what can I do?"

"You could have done a lot of harm to Feisul's cause by strengthening Saoud the Avenger," Grim answered.

"It is true that the French will turn Feisul out of Damascus; they are determined, he already suspects it, and I know it."

"*Mashallah!* What a wise one! How do you know it?"

"It is my business to know things," Grim answered. "Some men know about religion, others about the sea and tides; some study machinery; others know when camels will have young, and whether the price of wheat will rise or fall.

"I know about the intrigues of certain Governments. And as a trader looks for safety in a falling market, anticipating the day when it will rise again, so I foresee the outcome of intrigue and look beyond it and make ready. It is true that Feisul will be turned out of Damascus."

"Then why work any more for him? The hide of a dying camel isn't worth much. Why not look elsewhere — for instance, toward Saoud the Avenger?"

"Because Feisul has a host of friends, of whom I am one; and a loyal one," Grim answered. "Feisul will return, and the wise ones will make ready for him. There is all Mesopotamia and most of Arabia waiting to be welded into one. Who can do that except Feisul?"

"But the Avenger —"

"If he were strong enough, would set himself up against Feisul when the time comes. And of the two, which is the better man?"

"*Wallahi,* Feisul!"

"Then, why strengthen the Avenger? If, when Feisul comes, there should be two chiefs in these parts, neither of them strong enough to defeat the other, Feisul may make peace between them and secure the loyalty of both."

Ibrahim ben Ah's glittering, calculating eyes opened wider again, and his lips showed traces of a smile.

"And those," Grim went on slowly, "who have worked for Feisul will be reckoned Feisul's friends when his star rises. Which would you rather be reckoned — a friend of the Avenger, or of Feisul?"

"*Wallahi,* of Feisul!"

"I also. So we are agreed again. Now which is a man's friend — he who forgets and deserts him for the stronger side when foreign Governments break promises and betray him; or he who remembers, and watches, biding the time when the star that set in the West shall rise in the East again?"

"But you have separated me from my men. *Mashallah!* What use am I now to Feisul or any one?"

"Well," Grim answered, "I'll be frank with you. I didn't separate you from your men. My intention was to let Ayisha make good her boast that she can lead you by the nose."

Ibrahim ben Ah laughed scornfully at that.

"The woman Ayisha lied!" he retorted. "Now and then she has brought me messages from Ali Higg, and I have obeyed the messages, but not the woman. If she were Jael, that might be different. But Jael sent me word saying that the Lion has divorced Ayisha. If she had tried to lead me by the nose, I would have made a present of her to the first man who cared to feed the *bint!*"

"Yet, you see," said Grim, smiling pleasantly, "how Allah makes all things easy! I had in mind, as well, to rescue my two friends from your possibly dangerous society. They had no instructions from me to bring you away with them; yet Allah is all-knowing, and it seems it was not written that you should tell your men about the woman Ayisha's divorce.

"But it was written that my friends should so admire you as to crave your further company and cause you to be my guest for a while. I didn't expect it; but who am I that I should refuse hospitality to a friend of Feisul's?"

"*Shu hashsharaf!*" Ibrahim ben Ah exclaimed sarcastically. "You are possibly a worthy host, but I have called you hard names. Do you mean to swallow them?"

"I shall give you a chance to withdraw them before I speak of swallowing. What a man says in anger, being ignorant of all the facts, should form no part of the reckoning between host and guest, or between two friends of Feisul."

"And if I will not withdraw them?"

"We shall see."

Ibrahim ben Ah looked slowly around at the faces of our Arabs, who were listening as breathlessly as children at a play. Unseen by Grim, old Ali Baba tapped the bolt of his rifle with a threatening forefinger. Ibrahim ben Ah decided to consider matters further before definitely turning down Grim's offer of friendship; he judged the alternative might be swift, and far from sweet.

"But if you are Jimgrim," he said, "where is Ali Higg? And who can the Jimgrim be who sent me a warning at dawn? There must be two of you, for you came from the north, whereas the other disappeared toward the south."

"That other," Grim answered, "is Ali Higg himself pretending to be me."

"*Mashallah!* Why?"

"Presumably to draw off some of the Avenger's men."

Ibrahim ben Ah nodded. The virtue of that piece of intrigue appealed to him at once.

"A shrewd plan!" he commented. "I see how that could be done. There was a day when Jimgrim, having Government remounts in charge, disobeyed an order and sent five hundred camels to Saoud the Avenger. So if Jimgrim, pretending to be in distress, sends to the Avenger now for a loan of five hundred men for a few days — yes — I see the merit of that plan. With only three or four hundred left to him the Avenger might be taken unaware and defeated easily. I see."

Grim smiled broadly.

"Let us hope he does succeed in decoying five hundred men," he answered. "I hardly think the Avenger will prove quite so generous as that. But even so, do you think one hundred and forty or so could defeat the number the Avenger would still have?"

"*Inshallah,* if Jimgrim had a hand in it."

"I'm afraid you're a flatterer," said Grim, "or else you think better of Ali Higg's ruffians than I do. No, there's going to be no battle with the Avenger."

"You will be a clever one if you can prevent it," Ibrahim ben Ah retorted. "The Avenger is already on the move."

"So is Ayisha," answered Grim. "And so shall we be in twenty minutes."

Once more Ibrahim ben Ah's gesture and attitude betokened resignation to inevitable fate.

"Who am I that I should understand such craziness!" he exclaimed. "Let the Avenger come then, and eat up the land like the locust. It is Allah's will."

"I know the heart of Feisul, and I understand a little of the heart of Ali Higg," Grim answered. "I can guess the course of Saoud the Avenger. But the will of Allah is something I can not divine. I am no prophet. Perhaps you are?"

"Nay, nay! I never said it."

"Then we neither of us know the will of Allah, and we are agreed again. That makes three points of agreement. Let us see if we can find a fourth."

"*Taib.* Let us see."

"Feisul will be turned out of Damascus by the French, and will go to Europe. Later he will return and be made ruler of all this country, or at least of the greater part of it. When that day comes, would you like to be on the side of the Avenger, and so obliged to oppose Feisul?"

"No."

"Would you eat the Avenger's salt now, and betray him afterward when Feisul comes?"

"Nay; why should I? But will Feisul come? I hear you say he will, but is that proof of it? *Wallahi!* A man might say with equal ease that the sky will fall on us."

"Nevertheless, you are a man of judgment, used to weighing words. Wild sayings in the mouth of one man are stark truth on the lips of another. Do I look like a fool to you? Look at these friends of mine. Do they look like fools? Would such men follow a mere babbler of vanities? And would I, think you, risk my life and the lives of my friends in this desert, paving the way for a man who is not positively sure to come?"

"Well, what is your bargain?" Ibrahim ben Ah asked dryly after a moment's pause, during which he examined Grim's face like a jeweler studying the works of a watch.

"I make no bargain," Grim answered. "I told you that. If you are a knave and a liar — a man untrue to his salt — forgetful of his friends — a mere desert jackal, changing sides at every opportunity, I will have nothing to do with you. If that is what you are, I will give you your camel and turn you loose, to die with the other jackals when your time comes."

"That is a hard saying," said Ibrahim ben Ah.

"Nevertheless, a true one," answered Grim. "But if you are a man true to his salt — a friend of Feisul — unwilling to betray the Lion of Petra without first giving him fair warning face to face, then I will make you an offer."

"*Wallahi!* You look like the Lion in countenance, but you talk like an honest fellow, Jimgrim! If the Lion had thy spirit, as he has thy face, I would never have considered leaving him."

"You can leave him now, if you wish," Grim answered. "None will prevent you. There kneels your camel. Take it, if you will."

"But Ali Higg is not for Feisul," Ibrahim ben Ah objected.

"Any man is for Feisul, who prevents the Avenger from growing too great and fouling Feisul's rightful nest," Grim answered. "So if you continue to serve Ali Higg, you will be working in behalf of Feisul until Feisul comes."

"But how can I serve Ali Higg without the army you have taken from me by a trick?"

"Just at present much better than with it."

"How?"

Grim turned toward Ali Baba with one of those business smiles of his that make you wonder why he isn't a millionaire, or at least the representative of one.

"Bring bread and salt," he ordered.

That took a minute or two, for one of Ali Baba's sons had to go and unfasten a camel-load and take the remains of breakfast from the top. Ibrahim ben Ah had plenty of time to weigh in his mind what was going to happen next.

"Your camel waits," said Grim. "You may go free. None will fire at you. There is no dishonor in refusing to eat salt."

But Ibrahim ben Ah made no move until Mohammed gave bread and salt to Ali Baba, who handed it in turn to Grim. Thus it had full significance — son's hand into father's; captain of the gang's hand into Grim's. It was official salt, produced under the eyes of witnesses.

Grim broke a piece of bread and dipped it in the salt in front of Ibrahim ben Ah, who followed suit. Each man ate his morsel in silence. Then —

"I have eaten thy salt, O Jimgrim," said Ibrahim ben Ah.

"I bear witness!" announced Ali Baba.

"I, with sixteen sons and grandsons, bear witness that Ibrahim ben Ah, commander of the host of Ali Higg, the Lion of Petra, has eaten the salt of Jimgrim."

"We bear witness!" they chorused after him.

"And now?" asked Ibrahim ben Ah, wiping his mouth on the back of his hand.

"I will show you how to turn a trick for Feisul," answered Grim. "You are a man, I take it, who loves truth?"

"None better. But the stuff is rare!"

"And I dare say it amuses you to tell the truth and see the fool who listens twist it to his own undoing?"

"That is the essence of all humor, Jimgrim. Aye, *wallahi!* I am good at that."

"And are you afraid to go to the Avenger?"

"*Tfu!* Why should I be? Has not the Avenger sent me messages to win me over to his side?"

"Then if it can be shown afterward that you served Ali Higg's cause well by doing so, so that after the event Ali Higg must needs trust you more than ever as a man of exceeding courage and wisdom in extremity, will you go to the Avenger and tell him truth with which he may confound himself?"

"By God, Jimgrim, you ask a lot, don't you?"

"Not a bit of it! I ask nothing. I offer you an opportunity. But if you are afraid —"

"In the name of the Prophet, on whom be peace, don't talk to me of fear, thou foreigner! If you, who are a stranger from a land of cursed infidels, can risk your bold neck for Feisul, am I less than you?"

"Let us admit you are the greater," answered Grim.

"*Taib.* It is nothing but the truth; for my men are a hundred and forty — yours but a score."

That was too much for Narayan Singh's self-control; he broke out into a smile such as you can see on the faces of the gargoyles of Notre Dame, or some of the temple images of India. And as for Ali Baba, there was no containing his disgust. "Jimgrim may admit what he pleases," he declared scornfully. "As for me, I am an insect under Allah's heel. But behold my sons and grandsons! There are not their like in all the continents! Are we only a score all told? Then we are better than a hundred score of dogs like thine!"

"Prodigies, no doubt!" said Ibrahim ben Ah.

"Aye, by Allah's favor, prodigies! Look at this one — my eldest-born."

He took Mujrim by the arm and pulled him forward.

"Have you such a giant in all your army of cattle-lifters? Look at him! Judge of his strength!"

"And here," he said, grabbing hold of me, "is one who had the better of him in a bout! These two alone could beat thy army of camp-scavengers!"

It was a relief to me to know that the old man had taken the defeat of Mujrim in that spirit; I had rather dreaded the outcome. But it isn't exactly comfortable to be led forth by the arm like a professional pugilist and have your horn blown by some one who can boast as he pleases and then leave you to make good the vaunts. As I've said, I enjoy a stand-up fight on equal terms, but there are limits.

However, Grim was fortunately in no mood for side issues of that sort. "We must get the better of a bigger force than Ali Higg's, and boasting beforehand isn't going to help much. Let us start now, and sing songs about it afterward."

HE SUITED action to the word by walking to his camel; but he did not mount until Ibrahim ben Ah had mounted — an act of courtesy that, I think, went a long way to confirm the old pirate's newly pledged friendship. What was more, he gave Ibrahim the place of honor by his side, and we had ridden up out of the ravine and traveled several miles in a more or less southerly direction before I had any chance to talk with him privately.

At last, though, Ibrahim ben Ah fell back with the perfectly obvious intent of satisfying curiosity by drawing into conversation whoever might feel disposed that way; and I seized the opportunity to range alongside Grim.

"You're the Devil," said I, and he laughed.

"How so?"

"I've had how many adventures with you? Quite a number. All the while I've supposed you were a sort of volunteer policeman, satisfied to keep the peace and let history shape itself."

"So I am."

"Not you! I've found you out. What beats me is why you never told me you're gunning for Feisul all this time. I know Feisul," I said, "and I like him. He assays pounds to the ton of pure gold. Why in thunder couldn't you tell me that all this lonely, dangerous business is in Feisul's behalf? I'd have been twice as keen."

The hot wind was excuse enough for not answering at once. There came a sudden blast of it that whirled the dust into our faces, obliging a man to tuck his chin down into the face-cloth and lean forward.

But he was silent for several minutes after the squall had passed. For he is a strange fellow; I think it strains him somewhere inside to be obliged to make confession of his deepest thoughts.

He is the exact opposite, in fact, of a propagandist. I think he feels that the airing of desire and parading of convictions are indecent. He smiles at other men's and makes a secret of his own. To some extent, too, he treasures ultimate purpose as if its very secrecy were half its strength, permitting only momentary glimpses of it under the stress of circumstance.

"You wouldn't have been half as keen," he said at last. "Tell me why you have come as far as this with me."

I chewed the cud on that before I answered. Few men can explain their real motives at a moment's notice.

"Because I consider you a white man who can show me sport," I answered after a minute.

"Have you changed your mind?" he answered.

"No."

"But if I had told you in the first place that I'm bent on putting Humpty-dumpty back on a wall that he hasn't been knocked from yet, you'd have put me down as a visionary; and, even supposing you'd still come for the sport of the thing, you'd have hung back all the time, and argued; and sooner or later you'd have discovered that your own affairs are more important to you than my dreams."

"But I've told you I like Feisul," I said.

"All right. Has your discovery that I'm working for him changed your judgment in any way?"

"Of course not. I'm glad to know that you think as highly of him as I do."

"Well, then, what's the trouble?"

"I'm not troubled. I'm interested. You're the first man I ever met who had a cause and wouldn't talk about it. Most men get on soapboxes, or into pulpits, or sit at a desk, and yell."

"Let 'em!" he answered. "Any man may waste his time who feels like it. I don't like noise, and don't believe it gets you anywhere.

"Each man's opinions are his own affair; goats, sheep, rats, camels, fish have opinions, too, I dare say. I have mine, but I don't inflict 'em on other folk. Who was it said we're faced by circumstances, not by theories?"

"Very well," I answered, "here's a circumstance. If you had told me to begin with that you are out for Feisul, I would have jumped at the opportunity to help."

"Seems to me you've helped quite a bit as things are," he answered smiling. "But anyhow I hate that kind of thing — despise it! No man has any right to cajole me into risking my life, or risking anything else for that matter, in his cause. I've no right to play such a dirty trick on you, or anyone. You wanted adventure. You asked for it. Have I proved a niggard host?"

"Ha-ha!"

"Besides, I'm out for Feisul with reservations. It's not my job to foist him on to the Arabs. That's up to them. I saw them root for him during the war, and after the armistice. I've watched every underhanded, dirty, low-down trick in the process of getting rid of Feisul from outside; and if I loathe anything on God's green earth it's control of other people by so-called interests. I'm more against the foreign politicians than for Feisul.

"If Feisul can come back, and the Arabs still want him, I'll do my bit to make things easy for him and them, that's all. I won't preach for him. I won't argue. I won't betray the uniform I sometimes wear, or the Administration that pays my salary. But when I come across people here and there, who happen to think the same way I do, and want to see Feisul back, I'll work with them like a beaver, and that's all."

It seemed about enough to me. I made up my mind there and then to let private affairs in America go hang, and to see Grim through on his rather original, perhaps Quixotic, quite unselfish, and possibly unprofitable quest.

CHAPTER IX

"Should I stoop to a pig-Pathan, with a prince waiting for me?"

THERE are two outstanding peculiarities of that ancient land of Edom, wherein we were adventuring; for that matter, they apply to all Arabia, most of Palestine and Syria, and to the desert places in between that are any man's land or nobody's according to the seasons, and disease, and the ebb or flow of politics.

One is that warfare is governed and restricted absolutely by the water-holes. An army can move only from one hole to another, as in a game of checkers.

Consequently a man like Allenby, who was daring enough to import American iron pipe and pump his water supply along behind the army, was able to upset all calculations. The Turks swore first and last that it wasn't fair, and the German General Staff agreed with them. Failing an efficient force of modern engineers, whoever makes war in the desert moves by water-holes. The other outstanding feature is a mental peculiarity of the inhabitants. They are first-class fighting men in most ways, but utterly unreliable when reporting numbers. Not even the Bulgarian general staff, when counting prisoners of war, was half as wild in its estimate as any Bedouin invariably is when speaking of his own force or the enemy's.

Tribes that can put seventy rifles in the field boast glibly of seven hundred. Opposed to a hundred men, they will describe them as a thousand; and after a victory will sing about ten thousand — which perhaps accounts for some of the swollen returns in Old Testament history.

We knew the strength of Ali Higg's force, now led by Ayisha, pretty accurately. A hundred and forty was about the right figure. But Saoud the Avenger probably believed them to be seven or eight hundred at least; and he may have supposed them more numerous than that.

It followed that, although the Avenger's force was reported to number eight hundred rifles and a thousand camels, that estimate might safely be cut in half by any conservative strategist. Probabilities are dangerous things to play with, but it was no worse than a fair guess that the Avenger had with him in the field twice or three times the number of men that we could dispose of, but no more.

A little army like that, however, can swell in numbers after a victory in much the same way that a mountain torrent overflows its banks. So if the Avenger should by any stroke of fortune or flash of generalship outmaneuver Grim, hundreds more from scattered settlements were likely to flock to his standard within a day or two; and to feed them he would have to carry on, seeing there is no such food-consuming, unproductive Frankenstein monster as a victorious army that sits still.

We soon were to have a chance to form our own estimate of the real strength of the rival forces. In front of us was a sugar-loaf hill, cut sheer on the northern side. Grim led straight toward it.

In the distance on our right, cut off from us by two or three deep *wadis* and a waste of rock-strewn sand, was Ayisha's column kicking up a cloud of dust like the smoke-trail of an ocean liner.

We left our camels at the foot of the sugar-loaf hill — where there wasn't a vestige of water, by the way — and Ibrahim ben Ah, Mujrim, Ali Baba, Narayan Singh, Grim and I struggled painfully to the top on foot. The rocks, and even the sand in places, were hot enough to burn you through the soles of thick shoes.

From the top we had a good view of Abu Lissan in the distance — apparently a cluster of mud and stone roofs, with a minaret or two and a good-sized patch of green that betokened date trees.

"Good plundering yonder!" was Ibrahim ben Ah's sole comment as soon as he had recovered breath.

Ali Baba and Mujrim echoed him. It didn't look like good anything to me from that distance; a more discouraging landscape, or a meaner lot of squalid buildings, wouldn't be very easy to imagine. But I suppose such experts in the art of acquiring other men's belongings would know where to dig for treasure that the mean surroundings were deliberately planned to mask.

We could see for many miles in every direction — even as far as the *fiumara* behind us, in which we had camped the previous night. The hill, with three wells in the crook of its elbow, where Ayisha had taken charge and we had made a "guest" of Ibrahim ben Ah, cast a long blue shadow to our right rear.

Over on our left, extending in a ridge like a monster's backbone for endless miles until it ran into the sky at the horizon, lay one of the mountain chains of Edom, with a much lower, broken range at its feet, running very nearly parallel, so that the two were like a double earthwork on a titanic scale. In two or three places many miles apart between breaks in the lower range were patches of bright green, indicating water.

From that mountain range, all the way across our front as far as Abu Lissan, was dry desert, blown here and there into humps like a camel's. At a guess, that part of the plain was fifteen miles across, measured in a straight line from Abu Lissan in any direction, so that the town, which itself was a smirch on the face of a hillside, stood as it were a hub in the center of a half-wheel, because the chain of hills on our left had a pronounced curve.

The nearest water-hole to Abu Lissan that we could see from where we stood lay about five miles away from us on our left hand. No buildings were visible, but there were enough trees to suggest ample supplies of water; and it was obvious at a glance that an army advancing on Petra would have its choice of two routes.

The longer, northwesterly way on our right hand, as we stood facing Abu Lissan, would lead by the wells where Ibrahim ben Ah had bivouacked. That to the northeast, on our left hand, would follow the foot-hills, providing water at the end of fifteen miles, and a further scant supply in the bed of the *fiumara* in which we spent the night.

A commander might divide his force for sake of the time that he would save at the water-holes, sending half his men by either route, rendezvousing in the *fiumara* for a march on Petra. Alternatively, any one attacking Abu Lissan might converge simultaneously from two water-holes, and be secured against that bugbear of an army, a congested, dry line of retreat.

THE Avenger had seized the water-hole to our left, for we could see an advance guard of his camel-men taking it easy there. Grim swore he could make out a machine-gun through the glasses, and Ibrahim ben Ah confirmed that with a discouraged nod. But as Narayan Singh said promptly:

"A machine-gun in the hands of such folk works while it is new. Thereafter it impedes them, for they wait on it, and dance about it, and swear, and pray; and then, because it continues jammed, they waste time trying to hide it from the enemy, who naturally make it as hot for them as possible. And presently, because their faith was in the machine-gun, they lose courage and run. I know; for I have seen."

Another force of the Avengers, of, I should say, two hundred men, was advancing leisurely behind a sand ridge two by two, to join the advance guard at the water-hole. We could see their heads and their spears and rifles over the top of the ridge. They might be going to spend the night at the water-hole — for they don't as a rule make a long march on the first day out — or possibly they intended to rest there, and make a forced march by night on Petra, which in that case would bring them into the entrance gorge somewhere about dawn. We looked for a long time before we detected signs of the Avenger's other wing, which as a matter of fact had started on its way toward the three wells by which Ibrahim ben Ah had bivouacked. For several minutes we could not even make out Ayisha's column, which had taken cover far to our right in a *wadi.* She had placed nine or ten men on a high mound near its rim to keep watch, and they lay low; but the sun gleaming on their rifle-barrels gave the clue to the column's whereabouts.

The men of the Avenger's left wing had caught sight of Ayisha's column before it entered the *wadi,* and themselves had taken cover amid a cluster of rocks and sand-hills near the middle of the plain below us to our right front. They were extremely well hidden, being difficult to make out even from our height looking downward.

They were evidently waiting for instructions. A thing that looked like a bedbug moving at amazing speed resolved itself with the aid of Grim's glasses into a camel-man riding Hell-bent-for-leather toward Abu Lissan. So it was a fair presumption that the Avenger hadn't left headquarters yet — a presumption that strengthened the other, that the whole force had intended to bivouac for the night at the two water-holes.

And now another hypothesis developed into something like a fact. Unless the Avenger had several hundred men remaining with him in Abu Lissan, of which there was no sign, or unless he had sent a raiding force away in another direction, which was unlikely, considering the task in front of him of tackling the hitherto invariably successful Ali Higg, then the total number of men he could dispose of dwindled already to five hundred at the outside estimate.

The two bodies of camel-men were close enough to be considered one force, since either of them could race to the assistance of the other in the event of a surprise attack. But it was pretty clear, nevertheless, that Ayisha's appearance on the scene with a compact force of a hundred and forty, which probably looked twice as big to their nervous imagination, had considerably upset calculations.

You see, the Avenger had done all the boasting. It was he who had pronounced damnation on Ali Higg, declaring him a heretic, which is the perfect form of propaganda in all Moslem lands. It was the Avenger, not Ali Higg, who had promised conquest and loot — women and gold and camels — the swift, tumultuous triumph for which the Bedouin's heart burns. So it was naturally disconcerting to find Ali Higg's men first in the field — and on their flank at that, instead of in a trap between the two wings of the Avenger, where a reasonable enemy ought to be.

Ibrahim ben Ah began to grow excited, and old Ali Baba seconded him. "Now, Jimgrim! Send a message to Ayisha quickly. Bid her attack at once. Those cowards of the Avenger's don't know what to do. They'll run, and be slaughtered.

"Then, having dealt with them as they deserve, we can cross the plain and show those others how brave men tackle a machine-gun. Quick now! Let me go!"

"Aye, let him go!" agreed Ali Baba. If I had stood in Grim's shoes I would have done just that. But Narayan Singh sat still on a rock and watched Grim's face; and Grim said nothing for a while — only kept on smiling. The more those two old firebrands clamored, the more set he seemed to be doing nothing, and on saying less. Ibrahim ben Ah actually clutched his arm at last, and shouted in his ear:

"Allah sends such opportunity but once in a man's life! *Allaho akbar!* Say the word, Jimgrim, and a hundred men shall overwhelm a thousand!"

"There's not going to be any fight," Grim answered at last.

"But we could win easily!"

"Maybe. Perhaps. But one fight breeds another. There's a better way of settling this." He turned to Ali Baba. "Call up those sons of yours from down below, old fox."

That suited the old man perfectly. He was a fanatic about those sons and grandsons. No plan could fail, in his opinion, if they were linked up with it; and he retained the courage of conviction in spite of the fact that if you added up their jail sentences it would need a Methuselah to contemplate the lot with equanimity. He went to bellow to them, making a trumpet of his hands, and in a minute they were swarming uphill.

"Let's hope the Avenger has a field-glass," said Grim.

And that was no wild-cat suggestion, because during the great war nearly all the Arab commanders in the field became possessed of things of that kind, either in the form of loot from Turkish and German officers, or as presents from the Allies.

Twenty-one men, all armed with rifles, can make a fairly good showing over half a mile of hill-top, if they move about enough. We spread out in both directions, dodging behind boulders, sometimes running, sometimes walking across the open; and then, as if Grim were directing the making of a motion picture, retiring out of sight to form platoon, march in and out of view, reform into single line to look like a different body of men, and finally disappear.

A T THE end of half an hour we had accomplished one thing anyhow. Both wings of the Avenger's men had seen us. Evidently they did not have field-glasses, or the shorter range would have betrayed the trick. The men advancing toward the water-hole began to hurry forward, and those already waiting there collected their camels and took close formation.

"Now for the awkward half an hour!" said Grim. "We win or lose now on the strength of what the Avenger ate for breakfast. If he felt good, and sent his brightest man away with the right wing, we're done for. We'll have to call Ayisha off, and scoot for the tall timber. Any wing commander worthy of his salt would send scouts now to look behind this hill. But if the Avenger didn't feel good, and kept his brightest man by, handy to advise with; and if, on top of that, he's got news of a certain Jimgrim snooping somewhere to the southward — Lord knows what the Lion's doing, but it's certain he's pretending to be me — then that left wing may rest satisfied that we're a strong force, and wait for orders. The Avenger may decide to recall 'em all, and watch points."

It was then that Narayan Singh gave proof of his military judgment. As I have said, he is fit to command a brigade, if only a brigadier in these exacting days didn't have to stay sober all the time.

"Why leave it to their judgment, *sahib*?" he growled out.

He can't speak gently about military matters, but thrusts out his jaw and looks savage.

"We are one-and-twenty men. That is a scouting force big enough to represent two hundred men at least. If we go scouting they will draw their horns in, thinking we are likely an advance guard sent to force a fight."

"Right you are!" Grim answered. "You usually are right. If they should call the bluff we'd be no worse off than if they'd sent their own scouts out to investigate us."

But even so it was a risky business. Too much depended on the temper of the Avenger's men, and on what instructions he had given them. All we had to count on was the psychological effect made on them by surprise at finding what they supposed was a strong force.

But there never was a plan of any sort, since Adam was booted neck and crop from Eden, that hadn't its Achilles' heel, and its moment when success depended on the other fellow's doing the wrong thing. Otherwise we'd all have been back in Eden long ago.

We clambered down the hill, mounted our camels, and swooped out suddenly on the plain, going at a fast clip in close formation for the first mile. Then we opened out to fifty yards or so apart, just as a precaution in case that machine-gun should be really in working order.

We had one indisputable advantage. The splendor of old Ibrahim ben Ah's raiment, and the red-and-blue trappings of his camel, proclaimed him from a long way off as a person of distinction; such individuals don't lead scouting or skirmishing parties as a rule unless there is a strong supporting force within hail.

Moreover, we were all magnificently mounted; the points of a camel are the first things that appeal to a Bedouin's eye; and, just as a good store window suggests opulence within — without necessarily insuring it, so the perfect turn-out of a force of scouts implies a well-found, numerous army in its rear, notwithstanding the uncensored, open pages of the Chronicle of Bluff.

But, as I said, it was a risky business. They actually started on its way a force of twice our number to ascertain our intention; and Ibrahim ben Ah, lifelong follower of desert tactics, shouted to us to scatter and run.

But Grim is a first-class poker player, and not addicted to throwing down his cards just because some one across the table has raised him a hundred per cent. He sent Ali Baba's youngest grandson scurrying back alone toward our sugar-loaf hill, as if to bring out re-enforcements, and led straight on.

You remember how the stars in their courses fought against Sisera? Well, the sun was out, so I can't vouch for the stars; but the kites and eagles came to our assistance.

We had left our baggage-camels hobbled among boulders at the rear of the hill; and I suppose, not liking to be left behind, they had called attention to themselves by struggling to get up. They may have looked from the upper realms of air like dying animals. I can't vouch for that either.

But I do know that three or four eagles, at least a dozen vultures, and kites by the score began circling above them with a meal in view. What more could you ask for to establish the presence of a considerable force of men?

So the oncoming skirmishers retired before us without coming close enough to make an exchange of shots worth anybody's while. And at about that moment the galloper came hurrying back from Abu Lissan with orders for the other wing. They sent men to meet him, to save time.

There was an exchange of signals, and the Avenger's left wing left cover in a hurry, smoking back for the town with a devil-take-the-hindermost appearance, which may or may not have been deceptive. And as the hindermost were mostly baggage-camels laden to capacity, it was all Grim could do to restrain Ali Baba from leading his gang of thieves in hot pursuit.

"Why should Allah make things easy, if we refuse to help ourselves?" he demanded with pious wrath.

But he is a loyal old fox, and gave in, fuming, when Grim made his veto sufficiently emphatic.

The sudden retreat of the left wing was the last straw that convinced the Avenger's right. They packed up their precious machine-gun and departed from that water-hole of one accord and with one mind; and the dust of their going, caught up in a blast of the simoom, was like the smoke-screen of a fleet in action.

One thing that was no news in the dawn of history, but that the Allies had to learn all over in the great war, is that, though Arabs are like a steel-shod tempest in attack, coming on as if welcoming death to the roar of their *"Allaho akbar,"* you can't stop them when they once start running.

Then they're like steers in a stampede; the camels seem to catch the frenzy of their riders, and the whole lot go scurrying helter-skelter for the hiding place nearest to home. Some even actually do go home, disregarding the runaway's prerogative of coming back to fight another day.

So we found ourselves possessed of that oasis in the gap in the lower range of hills; and since the dust kicked up by their retreat rendered us perfectly invisible to the Avenger's men we made our way to it leisurely, most of us roaring with laughter and exchanging jokes.

Only one thing seemed to worry Grim now. There was a serious danger that Ayisha might not be able to restrain her men from following the general retreat with a view to plunder.

Although that would certainly have turned disorder into utter rout, it would have just as certainly brought on reprisals as soon as the Avenger should have rallied his runaways in Abu Lissan. Reprisals were the last thing Grim was looking for.

He sent Mujrim at top speed to find Ayisha, with orders for her to leave twenty men under a picked captain, who could create an appearance of numbers, and to bring the rest of her force, under cover all the way if that were possible, to the rear of our sugar-loaf hill.

That attended to, he examined the oasis; and it was a sight to gladden the eyes of any man with a problem such as his not yet more than half-solved. There was an ample supply of water for a force a dozen times the size of ours, but that was almost the least attraction.

There was firewood by the camel-load, by the cord, by the ton — heaps and piles and mounds of it. A hundred women working for a month under their impatient husbands' eyes could hardly have cut that quantity.

The Avenger was evidently a foresighted conqueror. Having seized Abu Lissan and decided to make it the pushing-off place for a more ambitious campaign, he had sent firewood parties up into the hills to lay in a good store of the stuff. For firewood in any quantity is about the hardest thing to come by when campaigning in that sterile land, and doubtless the Allies had taught him in the war the benefit of getting stores piled up ahead.

Whether he had intended to transport the stuff to Abu Lissan, or to relay it by camel-loads behind his advancing army, was none of our affair. There the wood was, mostly bound together in negotiable bundles, and it was worth to Grim in that minute incalculably more than all the loot that might have been picked up by following the retreat of the Avenger's men.

J IMGRIM measured the stuff with his eye and began to hum tunes to himself. He lit a cigarette, and whistled. He threw the cigarette away, seized hold of me, and danced a two-step all in among the piles of wood. Finally he stripped himself and took a bath in the small rock basin over which the spring bubbled musically.

When Ibrahim ben Ah requested an explanation, he sang him a little song in English about a "merry man moping mum, who asked no sup and who craved no crum, and all for the love of a la-a-a-dy." Then he climbed to the top of the hill behind, to sit and watch for Ayisha; not that any of us doubted she was coming, but that Grim wanted to form his own judgment as to whether or not the movement of her column could be seen from Abu Lissan.

Narayan Singh and I rode back then to the sugar-loaf hill to bring along the baggage-camels, for all our eatables were stowed in the loads; and if exercise, excitement and amusement do a thing to you at all, they make you hungry. I hate a diet of uncooked dates for more than two meals in succession; they're handy and all that; they'll keep you alive, and still be palatable after they've been sat on in the hot sun; yet I've noticed that the Arabs, though they boast of them, agree with me in eating in preference almost anything else that comes along.

And we had canned stuff in the camel-loads — cheese and honest coffee and good wheat bread. Have you tried wheat bread in cans? It keeps "new" for months, and there's nothing like it to campaign on.

Narayan Singh was in one of his moralizing moods. He often gets that way when something he admires takes place under his eyes, and there is time to turn the various aspects of it over in his mind.

"There is no such thing as a color-line, *sahib!*" he exclaimed suddenly, at the end of a quarter of a mile. "Nevertheless, we dark men draw it more determinedly than you white men do. But that is craziness.

"There are two sorts of men; no others. Men who naturally can. Men who can't. Jimgrim can; and there you have him. I have fought under generals who can't; and believe me, that is a costly business for the rank and file.

"There are some men to whom you could give kingdoms, and they would lose them in a week. There are others, whom you could strip as naked as a little frog — as Jimgrim was in the pool just now — and if you turn them into the desert naked, they will carve a fortune or change the country's face.

"Our Jimgrim hasn't fired a shot, and I wager he will fire none. He hasn't told his plan, and I wager he never made one. He can; and he knows he can. He goes forth; and fortune goes with him. Can you tell me the why of that?"

"Natural talent, I suppose. Training, environment, a liking for the task. I'm not good at conundrums."

"Neither am I, *sahib.* But I know this. There is a line that is not a color-line. Jimgrim is above the line, and we are below it. If you and I knew how to vault above that line, we might be green in the face with yellow whiskers, and nevertheless the world would change under our hands. By my beard and the Prophet of this people's feet, that Jimgrim of ours could be a king if he were minded — yet he would laugh at the idea, although I have heard it said that all you Americans regard yourselves as kings.

"He could be a millionaire if he were minded; yet I think he would regard the suggestion as a joke, although I am told that every other American looks on millions as his heritage.

"Jimgrim is a man of infinite capacity, who has nothing but a babu's salary. He enjoys everything, and wants nothing. He studies all manner of men, and is amused, but covets no man's shoes. Can you explain him?"

"Seems to me you've done it pretty well," I said. "Let's hurry. Come on. I'm hungry."

We had brought the baggage-beasts to the oasis, watered them, and started to prepare a meal before Ayisha came. She left her excited command behind the sugar-loaf hill and came galloping to confer with Grim.

Excitement was too mild a word for her condition; she was in her element, and as full of fiery zeal as Joan of Arc, although I dare say the glorious Joan had more compunction and less savagery. She looked lovely in her Bedouin costume, with eyes blazing and an Amazon smile on her lips; and she was too contented to resume her quarrel with me — actually tossing me a smile of recognition as she passed.

I did not hear what she said to Grim; they talked alone together by the pool; but what he said sobered her. She ate with us in silence, and the rest of us had to hustle to get our share, for her appetite wasn't what the old-fashioned finishing schools would reckon ladylike. She could wolf bread and cheese like a stone-crusher swallowing rock.

At last, with a mouth full of food, she sprang on her camel again and departed, just as the sun seemed to rest for an instant on the rim of the western horizon, as if it were a living ball of fire hesitating to make the plunge into the unknown. It was pitch dark by the time she reached her men.

Then began about the hardest work I ever lent a hand in. Grim and the rest of us — even old Ali Baba and Ibrahim ben Ah with his silken skirts tucked up about his waist — Ayisha and her men, and the camels all toiled harder than galley-slaves to get that wood distributed.

We laid it in great heaps at intervals along the hill-top at the back of the oasis. We carried tons of it to the sugar-loaf hill, and stacked it at even distances apart in long lines extending from each side of the hill, with a liberal supply on top — and the men who toted the loads up that hill had to be threatened each time they returned. We sent several tons on camel-back to the place where Ayisha had left her outpost. And we finished the job by midnight.

Lord! And weren't we tired then? I dare wager that not one man of all those Bedouins, nor even any of our seventeen beaver-active thieves, had ever worked half as hard; no, not if you added up all the work they had ever done, and set the total against that one performance.

Grim and Ayisha did the whip-work; Grim smiling, and seeming to be everywhere at once; Ayisha cursing, coaxing, laughing, laying on the stick — and they stood it from her, Heaven knows why! They didn't know of her divorce, and that meant something; they may have reckoned they must square accounts with Ali Higg if they struck back at her; and none of them got a close enough view of Grim in the dark to realize that he wasn't the Lion of Petra.

But there was more than that. She radiated and screamed courage; the spirit was infectious.

When the job was done, we spread and lighted the bonfires. And if the Avenger, watching from his roof in Abu Lissan, hadn't believed that there was an army camped against him then, he would have had less imagination than a piece of protoplasm in the radiolarian ooze.

Some of the men were told off to keep moving in the firelight; and, seeing the general theory of the thing now readily enough, they danced and sang. It was pretty easy to imagine the Avenger's feelings; added to the anxiety of having to face what he supposed was a force of at least a thousand men, there was the natural disgust at seeing all that good store of wood go up in flame. And of course, the more they danced around the fires, the more depressed he must have felt.

So FAR, good. A confident team is half the game; and a dejected opponent is a good proportion of the other half. But we had to be quick; for as surely as dawn should come the Avenger wouldn't have to exercise his talents much in order to discover the deception.

Grim called a midnight council under the stars, consisting of himself, Ayisha, Ibrahim ben Ah, Ali Baba, Narayan Singh and me; and he commenced proceedings by breaking his usual rule of not unfolding more than half of a plan at any time.

There wasn't anything to complain about on that occasion as far as frankness was concerned, although the plan would have suited *Huckleberry Finn* better than a man of my temperament. I like to be at handgrips with the details of a thing.

If it's to be a gamble, I prefer to see the cards dealt, as it were; and I'm constitutionally averse to any game in which there is a joker running wild. The joker was Ali Higg, the Lion of Petra. None of us could even guess what he was doing.

However, I was the only member of the party who did not view the whole plan with enthusiasm; and, having made up my mind not long before to back Grim to the limit, at least so long as I was playing his game, I kept my opinion to myself.

Ibrahim ben Ah surprised us all with his oath-embellished praise of the scheme. So much depended on him that I suppose Grim would have had to change the plan *in toto* if the old pirate had been half-hearted.

But he foresaw the opportunity of making a great name for himself as diplomatic peace-maker; and I think, too, that he wasn't without secret suspicion that circumstances might possibly develop in such fashion as would leave him standing in the Lion of Petra's shoes.

But nobody was half so enthusiastic as Ayisha. The names she called Grim would have made old King Nebuchadnezzar jealous. They made Ali Baba grunt contemptuously:

"*Wallahi!* I say that a woman's flattery and the voice of the devil are one!"

At that, chiefly for the sake of drawing Ali Baba, Narayan Singh came out with one of his ponderous jests:

"The woman's tongue tells no more than the triumph in her heart. Was she not alone and wretched? And is she not now loved to distraction by a Pathan of the Orakzai?"

He struck his chest as if it were a war-drum, and Ayisha almost spat at him. I think she would have, if Grim had not been between them.

"Should I stoop to a pig-Pathan," she sneered, "with a prince waiting for me?"

And she flashed her eyes at Grim in a way that made me almost as uneasy as Ali Baba was. What had Grim promised her? He was not the kind of man to break a promise. I didn't like the look of it, or of the triumph in her eyes. Neither did Grim's enigmatic smile look reassuring as he sat there silhouetted against the crimson of the nearest fire.

However, it was time to be up and doing, and the three of us whose task was to carry the first strategical assault examined our weapons and found our camels. Five minutes later, somewhere about one o'clock of a perfect, starry night, Ibrahim ben Ah, Narayan Singh and I rode out from behind the line of fires and headed straight for Abu Lissan, with Grim's last words resounding in our ears in Arabic:

"Peace ride with you! Remember our old friend Ali Baba's motto, 'Allah makes all things easy!' *Allah ysailmak! Tammu fi hiraset Allah!*"

CHAPTER X

"Wallahi!" And you say she has a following of fifty men?"

THE easiest thing in the world is to affect to look down on savages. We all do it. I've traveled, and looked, and listened; but I've never found the savage yet who didn't mock at some one whose emotions he considered more primitive than his own. I never got beyond the firework stage myself, and I'm free to admit that the sight of those bonfires in a wide horseshoe curve thrilled me more thoroughly than any row of old masters that I ever gaped at in a picture gallery.

Cultural standards are arbitrary anyhow, and mostly poppycock. A stark-naked aristocrat who had nineteen wives and no misgivings, up in the Nandi Hills beyond Kapsabit, once told me that I was an obvious Philistine because I blew my nose on a handkerchief. Ever since then I have chosen my own standard and gone forward under it; and I maintain — in the teeth of Rembrandt, Velasquez, Turner, and all the host who have amused themselves with paint — that what we had staged that night was Art. It was better than theirs, and there was more of it.

It was so good to look at, blazing irregularly up and down the outline of the hills, and in a straight, low string of crimson and orange splashes across the plain, that you couldn't feel afraid — even though we were quite likely riding to our deaths. It was gorgeous; it was full of color; it made the shadows dance; it suggested the titanic shapes of those raw hills.

And it was ours; we ourselves had done it. Even if another fellow had collected the material, it was we who spread that glowing paint.

Lord! How those fires did wink and dance behind us as we rode for Abu Lissan! I don't see how any man who wasn't a genius at divination could have guessed our force at as little as a thousand men. Knowing as I did how few we really were, I drew comfort from the sight of all those fires, and felt as if an actual army corps of friends was bivouacked in the hills. Far away over to our right there glowed a minor constellation, where Ayisha's outpost kept vigil; and if that didn't represent another thousand men at least, I don't see how any one in Abu Lissan was to know it.

But there was this to consider: The more afraid our fires had made the Avenger and his men, the greater the danger to us in approaching. Men in a panic fire wildly at the slightest sound.

Nor could we afford the time to creep up cautiously to the ruined walls and announce ourselves as white-flag bearers from some safe hiding place among the shadows. Grim had made no secret of the fact that we were taking a horribly long chance.

But I suppose our time hadn't come yet. Fortune favored us. Ibrahim ben Ah was, of course, a nominal fatalist by religion, and an opportunist by conviction and habit. I'm both or neither, I don't know which; except that, as I've said, "I've observed" that fortune favors the right side as a rule. Narayan Singh is a soldier, which is not a profession but a creed, whoever maintains the contrary; his viewpoint was peculiar to the sub-denomination that he follows:

"Many a man has stumbled on good fortune in the dark simply because he dared go forward. It is only they who wait for chances to whom chances never come."

Three points of view being superior to one apparently, we rode together into a perfect trap that proved to be our salvation.

The Avenger, scared though he was, had retained a modicum of common sense. We discovered afterward that he had tried to rally a skirmishing force that should unmask whatever might lurk behind those fires, but his men had threatened to mutiny at the first suggestion of it.

So he had had to content himself with minor precautions, and had managed to persuade a few score men that for the sake of their own skins it would be wise to go out on picket duty in the shadow of some sand-hills half a mile beyond the walls.

They were so appalled by our illuminations that they huddled all together in one dark spot. And they kept so quiet for fear of calling attention to themselves that we never even suspected their presence, or we could very easily have given them a wide berth.

As it was, they saw us, counted us, and held their fire, because bullets in the dark have a way of killing camel instead of rider. Camels taken alive are profitable loot; dead ones are only carrion. Dead men more often than not leave blood-feuds to be fought or settled with their relations whereas living prisoners may be held to ransom — besides which, you can cut their throats at any time.

So we were swooped on suddenly in the utter darkness of a gap between two mounds, dragged from our camels, and would have been disarmed if Ibrahim ben Ah hadn't found his tongue and the voice of authority. Age has its recompenses, even in the dark. They respected his age where they might have gagged and bound Narayan Singh and me; and once he had a hearing experience made him convincing. He called them sons of sixty dogs, of course. You begin most victorious arguments with that in Arabic. Then he cursed their mothers, wives, daughters and female relatives in general for several generations either way, before beginning on their fathers, brothers, uncles, sons and probable descendants — whom he pitied, because Allah wouldn't. He then called down a murrain on their cattle, and a desecration on their grandsires' graves, which he hoped would be used by imported sows as nests for raising families.

He was going on to tell them what would happen to their livers, hearts and kidneys in the world to come, when they implored him to desist, and asked him to explain what he was doing, and what he wanted.

So he assured them they were fools and heretics, without good sense in this world or any decent prospects in the world to come.

"Who but a son of a pig and a snake would dream of pulling *me* from a camel?" he stormed at them. "Who but the offspring of asses and thorns would suspect three men in such a place, riding straight forward, as possible enemies?

"Are ye the Avenger's men? *Wallahi,* he is well served! What will he say when he learns that his invited guest has been put to this indignity by the sons of his dung-hill builders in the dark under his very walls?" They were impressed, but still suspicious. They asked him for further information, and he gave it:

"Ye shall be crucified to the last man! Ye shall be flayed and beaten! Ye shall be cast to the kites, without a grave between the lot of you for the jackals to come and desecrate!

"Who am I? By Allah! Take me to the Avenger, and ask him who I am! Hear what he says, ye sons of promiscuous mothers!"

Whatever his generalship in the field, he knew those ropes all right. They gave him back his camel, and us ours as a natural corollary. They apologized. They begged a blessing from him to offset the curses he had showered so liberally. They promised him protection as far as the Avenger's door, and implored him to say a kind word for them to their tyrannical master.

Neither Narayan Singh nor I said one word during the whole interlude, which I dare say cost us ten valuable minutes, but introduced us without further trouble to the Avenger's front door. They gave us a guard of a dozen men, who rode before us shouting to the watchers on the walls to hold their fire; and the only opposition we encountered entering Abu Lissan was the snarling of about a hundred scavenger dogs that made enough noise to deafen you.

Ibrahim ben Ah was so careful to ride first, and so short with me when I called out to ask whether he had been hurt in any way when they dragged him from his camel, that I began to suspect him of contemplating a treachery. We were going to be hard put to it in that case to find a way of putting through Grim's plan, to say nothing of the individual risk to Narayan Singh and me.

But it was too late then to stop and catechize him, so we rode in through a dark hole that might have been a gap in a wall, or a gate, or the mouth of Hell itself, for all you could see of it. There were men on guard there, for we could hear them; and your nose informed you that the dogs hadn't attended to the sanitation any too efficiently. A backward glance at those reassuring fires of ours was the only comfort to be had.

There wasn't any reason that looked substantial just then why Ibrahim ben Ah should even regard as treachery the betrayal of Narayan Singh and me. True, he had eaten salt with Grim, not under duress, before witnesses; and likely had too high an opinion of himself to overlook that.

But Narayan Singh and I were in a different case. We had submitted him to violence, deprived him of his liberty, and — although we had been at pains to save his face for him before his own men — we hadn't spared his private feelings much on that occasion. He had eaten no salt with us two — an omission for which I felt inclined to blame Grim in the circumstances.

People who attach such high importance to the ceremony are almost always splitters of fine hairs when it comes to interpreting the spirit of agreements. He might easily consider it within his privilege to denounce us, while going through the farce of loyalty to Grim.

So I did a thing I have often done in advance of awkward situations. I put my pistol out of sight. If Ibrahim ben Ah intended treachery, then I also had a right to my intentions.

If any effort should be made to disarm me, I proposed to hand over my rifle, bandoleer and knife without any argument. Thereafter, whatever else might happen subsequently, Ibrahim ben Ah was going to get one nickel-coated bullet through the brain.

I would have liked to caution him, as a matter of fair play. But as that would have called his attention to the fact that I had hidden the pistol, it was out of the question. Besides, it was wholly up to him. He was in no kind of danger from me as long as he behaved himself.

I got a chance to whisper to Narayan Singh as we rode through the stinking, narrow streets; but there wasn't much that I could teach that man about taking care of himself. He had already hidden his revolver.

"If I am to die in this ill-smelling hole, the Avenger and some of his men will journey with me into the beyond, in addition to Ibrahim ben Ah!" he answered.

W E HALTED in front of a stout wooden door set deep in a solid wall; and evidently word had gone ahead of us, for we were admitted without a moment's delay, and were led up two flights of rickety stairs to a flat roof. The men who had brought us wanted to come too, but were driven down from the roof by three of the Avenger's staff with a storm of mixed invectives and reproaches.

The Avenger, armed to the teeth, was sitting near the center of the roof on a big chest covered with a rug. There was a lantern on a chair near by that showed his features clearly, and the first thing that struck me about him was that he was handsome, and not ill-natured.

The scar, of which Ali Higg had boasted as having spoiled his face, was there, but not nearly so prominent as I expected. Perhaps three inches long, it crossed his right cheek as far as the nose; and though the cartilage of his nose seemed to have been severed, he had either had good luck or else the services of a skillful surgeon, for it had healed pretty neatly.

For the rest, he was a dark-bearded man of middle height, with dark, lustrous eyes and splendid shoulders, who sat upright, with no apparent tendency to take things easy. He had a carved silver cigarette-box on the rug beside him, but no water-pipe; and though his dress was of fine material, there was no display of jewelry — no effeminacy. His hands were strong and well shaped, moving deliberately without unnecessary twitching of the fingers.

"*Salamun alaik!*" said Ibrahim ben Ah, bowing, very dignified.

He murmured something in reply, and asked why we had brought our weapons.

"Who should take them from us? I am Ibrahim ben Ah, commander of the camel corps of Ali Higg, the Lion of Petra."

"Do you come in peace?"

"I come under the rules of warfare, relying on your honor's honor. I come as a friend, if may be; but if my words find not approval, I shall ask permission to return as I came, unmolested."

The Avenger bowed his head slightly.

"Be seated. No, not in front of me; sit this way. There, now tell me what that means."

He did not point; in fact, he made no unnecessary gestures. He nodded in the direction of our bonfires in the distance, and I decided that I liked him. There was something fine and manly about his bearing and whole attitude.

The members of his staff were watching us from the stair-head with fingers on their triggers; but after that first question about our weapons the Avenger himself never referred to them again, nor acted as if he were aware of them.

"Who laid those fires?" he demanded.

"The Lion of Petra's men," said Ibrahim ben Ah.

"How many men has he then?"

"By Allah, I haven't counted."

"He has received a re-enforcement?"

"Behold! Surely a re-enforcement!"

"Whence?"

"God give your honor long life. I am not allowed to say."

"*Malaish.* From El-Kerak, I suppose, or possibly El-Maan. What have you come for?"

"*Inshallah,* to talk peace."

"Peace? Why peace, with such an army at your back? Peace is it, or treachery?"

"Your honor has favored me more than once with overtures by messenger. Your honor invited me to cross over with all my men and take service under you."

"You propose to do that?"

"God forbid! I have eaten the Lion's salt. Nevertheless, I am not your honor's enemy. It was fitting in the circumstances that I should carry offers of peace."

The Avenger glanced once, swiftly, at Narayan Singh and me.

"Why do you bring Indians with you?" he demanded.

That was Ibrahim ben Ah's opportunity, if he had any idea in his head of squaring personal accounts with us two. We were simply there to keep an eye on him. A polite request to have us tossed off the roof would most likely be complied with, after which he would still be in position to go through with Grim's plan. As for explanations afterward, who was likely to make much fuss about the lives of a couple of Indians?

The idea crossed his mind all right. He hesitated. Fortunately Narayan Singh and I were seated just a foot or so behind him, one on either side, in a line at right angles to the Avenger's seat and facing the suspicious staff. The Avenger himself wasn't looking, and none else could have seen the pistol that I thrust into Ibrahim's ribs under cover of my cloak, nor the revolver that touched a corresponding ticklish spot on the Sikh's side.

It may be possible to mistake the feel of a pistol muzzle on a dark night, but he didn't. He went straight ahead with the plan as Grim had outlined it, omitting nothing and introducing no personal vendettas.

"They belong to Jimgrim's force," he said in a hurry. "Jimgrim sent them as his representatives."

"Jimgrim?" exclaimed the Avenger, startled. "Where is the man? I had news of him from the southward; it was definite."

"He is this side of those fires," Ibrahim answered.

The Avenger glanced at me incredulously, but I confirmed the statement. If our plan was going forward, it was true.

"Why doesn't Jimgrim come and see me, instead of keeping company with such a dog as Ali Higg?" the Avenger asked suddenly. "I have nothing against Jimgrim. Why does he consort with my enemy?"

"He doesn't," I answered.

"Where is the Lion of Petra then — as the upstart calls himself?"

"Possibly Jimgrim knows, but we don't," I answered.

"Then is that army not marching against me?"

"At present it stands still," said I. "Jimgrim is doing his best to prevent hostilities."

"Why doesn't he come and see me?"

"He has not been invited; nor has he a safe-conduct."

"One of you go back and bring him. Let that day not come that shall see me refusing to confer with Jimgrim! He shall have fifty men to escort him safely through my lines, and if we do not agree together he shall depart in peace at dawn."

"Jimgrim has the task of restraining Ali Higg's army," I answered. "There is only one condition on which he will come."

"Name it."

"That you agree beforehand to make peace with Ali Higg, not on Ali Higg's terms, but on Jimgrim's."

"And if I refuse?"

"Then," said I, "your honor must deal with that army on your own responsibility. It will not be possible for Jimgrim to keep them waiting there many hours. It was only with difficulty that they were restrained from pursuing your honor's men a while ago.

"Hitherto they have listened to him, but he will dare to leave them only on the condition I have named. If your honor will put in writing an agreement to make peace on Jimgrim's terms, then he will come forward."

"But if he is on this side of the fires, how will that army know that I have yielded that point?" he asked suspiciously.

"If your honor will set it down in writing and hand the writing over to Ibrahim ben Ah, then it has been arranged that I shall make a signal that will be understood by all."

He sat in gloomy meditation for about five minutes before answering.

"What if I hold you three as hostages, and retire from Abu Lissan?" he asked suddenly.

That being a poser, it was my turn to meditate. None of us had an answer ready. I could have told him it would be a breach of faith to treat messengers in that way, but there isn't much to be gained, as a rule, by imputing bad faith in advance of the occurrence.

"That would not prevent pursuit," I said at last, "but it *would* lose you the good offices of Jimgrim."

"You mean he would —"

"I mean," I interrupted, "you would have to make what terms you could with your enemies, instead of signing peace on a friend's conditions."

"Conditions? What conditions will he make?"

"Who am I that I should answer that?" I replied. "You, who know Jimgrim, should be able to judge whether he will be fair with you or not."

"Jimgrim and I are brothers. He did me a favor once," he muttered half-aloud; then relapsed again into silence, and was silent for so long a time that I began to be nervous about the hour.

We had only until dawn to succeed; sunlight would show the skeleton on which our glittering display was spread.

"Try Jimgrim again," I suggested at last; and for answer he clapped his hands together.

One of the staff brought him paper and pen, and at Ibrahim ben Ah's dictation he signed a statement "in the name of Allah, the all-merciful, the compassionate" that he would agree to Jimgrim's terms if Jimgrim would come and hold the balance squarely between himself and Ali Higg.

He did not whine, squeal, wriggle, swear, seek to excuse himself, equivocate or make any fuss at all, but acted throughout manfully, ordering coffee to be brought as soon as he had signed the paper, and behaving generally like a gentleman, making the most of temporary failure. I was right glad to know he was being restrained from conquest that would inevitably bring him up against British artillery sooner or later.

I TOOK the lantern off the chair and swung it in a circle round my head for several minutes, until five shots from a pistol cracked out much nearer at hand than I had expected — so near, in fact, that I went on signaling, believing it could not be Grim.

But Grim, too, had been growing nervous about the hour, and had crept close in order to waste as little time as possible. The Avenger sent two of his staff to meet him and prevent accidents, and inside ten minutes Grim came up the stairs, not alone, but followed, of all improbable people, by Ayisha.

She hadn't been included in the plan as far as I knew; but Lord, how she was enjoying herself! What with her rifle and bandoleer, Amazon smile and blazing eyes, she looked as picturesque by lantern-light as any woman I have ever seen.

Grim stood smiling at the stair-head for thirty seconds, until the Avenger called out a sonorous greeting and rose to his feet to receive him. They seized each other's hands, and then embraced in the Arab style, which is Biblical.

"Once before, O Jimgrim, you came to my aid in a tight place. Do you bring peace now?"

"If you are swift," Grim answered, turning so as to face the undulating line of fires. "I can hold those men there until dawn — no longer."

"Let us talk then. I am in no shape just now to fight an army such as that. *Mashallah,* what locusts! They have eaten up in one night a year's supply of wood!"

Grim turned from admiring our illuminations, and sat down in front of him. Hassan Saoud the Avenger set both elbows on his thighs, and sat still, resting his jaws on the heels of both hands.

"Do you remember, at the time when I sent you those camels in the tight place you speak of, how I tricked you?" Grim asked him.

"*Wallahi!* Yes. Ha-ha! I never will forget it! It called for a cunning fox indeed to play that trick on me — and a wise one! I would have plundered Feisul's baggage but for you; and the Turks would have caught me in the bargain. That was a true Jimgrim trick; there is no other name for it."

"I'm going to trick you again," announced Grim.

"By Allah, I will take the chance," the Avenger answered, laughing. "Go ahead."

"I'm not joking. I want it clearly understood that I'm going to trick you. I shall take your word, Hassan Saoud, and hold you to it."

"I am no longer afraid of your tricks. I will pass my word as soon as we agree. It is several hours since I had the first inkling of this trick;

there came a message from the southward, saying that Jimgrim waited in a *fiumara* twenty miles away, and begged the immediate loan of four hundred men."

"What did you do about it?" Grim asked.

He did not look particularly interested; but Ayisha, standing upright in the dark behind Grim, leaned forward on her rifle with parted lips.

"*Wallahi!*" swore the Avenger. "It sounded like a strange request to come from Jimgrim. It sounded to me like a trap of some kind. So I sent fifty men, whom I could ill spare, and a man in charge of them who should have been commanding my right wing.

"Had he been with the right wing, there might have been another tale to tell about tonight's affair. My brother Achmet. You know him? Like a rifle bullet is Achmet for quick thinking. I said to Achmet:

" 'If the sender of that message truly is Jimgrim, than stay and serve him with your fifty. But if he is not Jimgrim, catch him and bring him hither, or else feed him to the jackals; but better to bring him alive, for the amusement we may have with him.' "

"It was very good of you, when you needed men so badly, to send your best wing-commander and fifty on the off chance of helping me," Grim answered gravely. "Let us call the account even between us, and begin all over anew."

"*Taib* — since you suggest it."

I began to feel horribly uneasy, and I know Narayan Singh did, for he was holding his breath and letting it out between his teeth sibilantly. I knew Grim was playing a hunch by the way he smiled and spoke slowly with his eyes not quite wide open; you learn to recognize a man's game after you have played with him a while and watched him in the climaxes.

But hunches are fickle friends. If the Lion of Petra should have been killed by the Avenger's brother, all our plan was worth nothing; and if he had been made prisoner, it looked like worse than nothing.

But Grim had to be quick. Before so very long now those fires of ours would begin paling in the dawn.

"Well then," Grim said slowly, "do you wish me to act arbiter in this dispute between you and Ali Higg?"

"Yes; for he seems too strong for me."

There was a long pause at that moment. Several shots were fired in the near distance toward the south. Shouting followed for two or three minutes; and then silence. I judged by the slow movement of his hands that Grim was horribly excited, but he had his voice under command.

"If I can call off that army then, will you agree to retire from Abu Lissan at once, and not to invade Ali Higg's territory for a period of three years?"

"Three years is a long time, Jimgrim."

"Nevertheless, my condition is three years."

There was another pause — the sound of a camel coming full pelt through the narrow streets — and then a disturbance in front of the door below.

"Make it one year, Jimgrim. I am a man of my word."

"Three years; or I wash my hands of the whole business."

The Avenger hesitated — stared at our fires for several seconds — seemed to review in his mind his own immediate resources — and was about to speak, when a brown-cloaked rifleman was ushered in a hurry up the stairs and advanced to deliver his message with hardly the form of salutation. He was out of breath, and brushed Ayisha aside as if he did not see her.

He was from the Avenger's brother. He reported that the person representing himself to be Jimgrim had tried to decoy him and his fifty men farther afield, but had been cornered, because he and his handful of men were mounted on dead-weary camels. At the moment of the messenger's dispatch the man, whoever he was, was parleying for terms, offering to surrender if his life was guaranteed him.

So the Avenger's brother had decided to grant that condition in order to save time; but there would be delay, because of those tired camels, which were, nevertheless, too good to leave behind. He hoped to bring in his prisoners before dawn, in time to take part in the offensive.

"Taib," said the Avenger, and dismissed him with a wave of the hand.

Ayisha went and sat down in the circle of lamplight, with an air that I mistook for resignation. Her face wore that fatalistic expression that you read about and very seldom see. Ibrahim ben Ah, looking rather triumphant and decidedly shrewd, whispered to Grim, who shook his head.

If you had asked me to play Grim's hand that minute, I would have thrown the cards down, for the arrival of Ali Higg on the scene as a prisoner of war would be a joker that would upset every calculation. Yet Grim looked uncommonly contented, and the Avenger, whose turn it was to deal, dealt the joker into Grim's hand.

"Inshallah, we shall have amusement, Jimgrim, when we confront you with the impostor!"

"Business before amusement, Hassan Saoud," Grim answered. "Will you agree to the three-year term of peace?"

"But if I agree, how shall Ali Higg be held to it? Will he give hostages? What proof will the scoundrel give that he intends to keep his word?"

Ayisha's eyes, that had been half-closed dreamily, opened wide at that, and the suspicion of a smile began to hover on her lips.

"Would a wife and fifty men do?" Grim inquired.

"The loss of fifty men would weaken him," said the Avenger.

"And the wife knows his affairs, knows his strength and weakness, and moreover involves his personal honor," answered Grim. "Do you not remember how the Prophet Mohammed required his follower Ali's wife as a token of allegiance? Would even Ali Higg dare to make himself a byword through all this land by breaking an agreement to confirm which he had given his wife before witnesses? If a man should lose his wife in battle, his honor would require him to seek revenge; but can he give his wife, and break faith afterward?"

"And what does he require of me?"

"Three years' peace."

"And at the end of that?"

"A lot can happen in three years," said Grim. "Let us plan for those, and leave the fourth in Allah's lap."

"Is the wife good-looking?"

"Judge for yourself," Grim answered; and Ayisha rose to her feet.

She looked less like a part of a bargain than the clever driver of one — dignified, alert, triumphant.

"*Wallahi!* And you say she has a following of fifty men?"

"There are fifty who are willing to change sides along with her and bring their camels."

"*Taib!* I agree."

"To what?" demanded Grim.

"To a three-year truce."

"Does that include personal immunity for Ali Higg? Do you undertake to lift no hand against him, and to take him at no disadvantage at any time during the next three years, beginning now, in return for a similar promise from him to you?"

"By Allah, why not? He marked my face; but I have his wife, and shall have fifty men! Yes, I agree. I promise. Why doesn't the dog show himself and sign the bargain?"

"He shall," said Grim.

"But when? Let my men go and bring him."

"Men have gone for him already," answered Grim. "He will be here presently. So you have passed your word? Between you and me, as man to man, in good faith? I may count on you to keep it?"

"In the name of Allah. By my beard and by the honor of my race," the Avenger answered.

CHAPTER XI

"I see no sin in holding to my given word. Let Allah judge me."

DAWN was just breaking when they brought in Ali Higg. Our beautiful row of fires was dwindling into dots of smokiness. I went through the farce of waving lantern signals to a phantom thousand men, although another twenty minutes was going to prove their non-existence; and we got in a row, staff-officers and all, to receive the prisoner.

I can't say which was more astonished — Ali Higg at sight of Grim, Ayisha and Ibrahim ben Ah, or the Avenger at discovering the prisoner's identity.

"By the Prophet's beard and my feet, this is a worse trick than I thought!" growled the Avenger.

And he glared at Ali Higg for several minutes, while his brother Achmet gave an account of the capture and what preceded it.

"He left a man in wait for us, by Allah, who swore that Jimgrim waited at a place ahead, whence he would lead us to Ali Higg's flank in such manner that his capture would be easy. But it sounded like strange talk to me; so I kept the man with me, and rode hard.

"We overtook this person who pretended he was Jimgrim. I passed my word not to kill him, and he surrendered. Lo! It was Ali Higg, who had thrown himself on my protection.

"He has not told me why Ali Higg should offer to betray Ali Higg by leading us on to Ali Higg's flank that we might capture Ali Higg — nor why he should call himself Jimgrim. Now make him tell.

"I promised him his life, but said nothing about torture. Moreover, there was nothing said about his men; if they were bastinadoed —"

"He only had a little private difference with me," said Grim. "I have the key to his private fortune in my pocket. As long as I have that he can't make war without losing fifty thousand pounds. I suppose his wife, Jael, persuaded him. It seemed simple to her to use the Avenger's men to waylay me. But Allah doesn't make all things easy for every one. Jael suggested, but the Lion of Petra bungled."

No one else spoke for several minutes. Ali Higg hardly resembled Grim any longer, for he was too dejected, besides being utterly fagged from the pain in his neck, his prodigious ride, and want of sleep. It would have been an act of charity to tell him to sit down, but the Avenger wasn't feeling charitable just then.

His face was black with anger, and the blackness deepened as he glared at the distant hills and began to realize the extent of the whole trick that Grim had played on him. There was smoke there now, and nothing else. The men had all disappeared behind the sugar-loaf hill, whence they could scoot for Petra at the first alarm.

Grim leaned forward at last, and took a cigarette from the

Avenger's silver box. He lighted it casually before breaking the silence, and then it was to Ali Higg that he spoke, not to the Avenger.

"O Ali Higg," he said, "I've made a bargain for you with Hassan Saoud the Avenger, who is a man of his word, although he doesn't like the bargain. There is to be peace between you two for three years. It extends to persons. His person is to be inviolable; so is yours.

"To bind the bargain, and in token of good faith, I have told him that you will give him your wife Ayisha, along with any fifty men who care to follow her fortune, camels and all. He undertakes not to invade your territory; you undertake not to invade his. This place Abu Lissan as far as both water-holes to the northward is to be neutral ground. Are you ready to sign?"

Ali Higg nodded. I think he was afraid that if he spoke he might wake up and find the good luck only a dream. He glanced once sharply at Ayisha, but made no sign to her — gave her no nod of recognition, although she met his eyes boldly.

At last the Avenger spoke, and in the dawn-light his face looked gray with grief and disappointment.

"I will sign the agreement with this dog who calls himself a Lion, Jimgrim; for I swore by Allah, and by the Prophet's beard, and by the honor of my race. I will take his wife, for she is good to look at, and has fifty men. The men will find better employment under me than under the Dog of Petra. *Taib.* Let a deed of peace be drawn accordingly, and I will sign it.

"But how about the issue between thee and me, Jimgrim? It was your suggestion that the account between us should be reckoned as balanced. Therefore we stand as two men not beholden to each other. As between you and me personally there has been no agreement made, nor oath passed, either as to your life or any other matter."

"Have one of my cigarettes," Grim answered calmly. "They're better than yours."

The Avenger waved the offer aside indignantly.

"I call myself Avenger. None has proven to me yet that that is not my name."

Narayan Singh's eye caught mine, and he patted the part of his cloak that concealed the revolver. I made ready, too; but Grim didn't seem in the very least disturbed.

"Very well, friend Saoud. I told you beforehand that I was going to trick you. If the account was even just now, let's admit that the balance between us has swung in your favor. I'm no more a *maskin* [poor sport] than you are. I'll consider I owe you a turn. How's that?"

"Such talk is easy. You have robbed me in the first place of a conquest; second, of a prisoner whom I would rather hold than any in Arabia; third, you have made a fool of me."

"Not so," said Grim, still smiling his seductivest. "I've made a fool of Ali Higg — saved you from destruction by a British army — provided you with a beautiful wife — and added fifty men with camels to your army, without your having to strike a blow for them. Now since you think the scales are still too low on my side, I say, 'Name your own makeweight'."

"By God, Jimgrim, your life would never be enough to balance this!"

"Of course it wouldn't. I'd be no use to you dead."

"By Allah, I have known revenge to taste sweet!"

It was in keeping with Grim's usual tact that he was silent on the subject of the British, who would certainly have exacted retribution, severe, though possibly indirect, from any sheikh who caused him to be slain. He chose a different line of argument.

"See here, Hassan Saoud, you're too fine a fellow altogether to give way to ill-temper now. Smile, and shake hands. You've got the right now to call on me in an emergency; I'll keep my word as well as you keep yours."

"You mean you will come if I call on you?"

"Inshallah," answered Grim. "I can't do impossibilities. But if you call, and it's possible, I'll come."

"And do as I bid you?"

Grim laughed aloud and reached for another of the Avenger's cigarettes.

"Here, take one of mine. No, you optimist! If I were to do what you told me to, we'd both be in a British jail within the week. What I do mean is, that if you're in a bad mess at any time, and if it's humanly possible, I'll come and help you out."

Well, that Avenger fellow was the nearest approach to a sportsman that I had seen yet in that part of the world, if you except our old fox, Ali Baba, and his sixteen performing thieves. He laughed, and decided to make the best of matters — in the teeth of opposition, too; for his staff officers and his brother Achmet argued for an hour, going so far at last as to produce a *m'allim,* very learned in Koranic law, who maintained stoutly that to fulfill any agreement imposed on him by the trickery of an infidel would be to set a bad example, and therefore sin.

"I see no sin in holding to my given word," he answered finally. "Let Allah judge me."

AFTER that all of us except Ayisha ate breakfast together on the roof — women don't eat with the men — and a devilish nasty mess it was, concocted of rice, powdered coconut, camel-butter, turmeric and the flesh of a goat that had been bleating less than an hour before.

The Avenger went through the form of eating salt with Ali Higg, but without enthusiasm, and insisted on referring to him as the Dog of Petra.

Then Grim drew up the agreement in triplicate, to which we all attached our signatures; and I don't know what law I broke, or what the penalty should be, but I set down an Indian name in the place reserved for me, and gave my address as Lahore, Punjab, India.

Since we were all dog-tired it was agreed that we should sleep the day through in Abu Lissan, and all of us go our separate ways that evening. Grim would have been quite contented to take the Avenger's word for our safety, and so would I; but when word was sent to Ali Baba about it, he turned up within the hour with his sons and grandsons, and insisted on their taking one-hour turns on guard.

"For men are like camels in this: That they dream dreams," he remarked dryly. "One who should dream that he was murdered while he slept might possibly not wake again."

So they spread rugs and mats on the floor of the long second-floor passage, and we sent up such a chorus of snores as I dare say that roof had never echoed to before. But I know the Avenger didn't sleep much, and don't suppose Ayisha did. The Avenger sat in conference in a small room with the *m'allim,* discussing all the intricacies of marriage to another man's wife.

Fortunately the Avenger had only three wives, and the Koran permits four; fortunately, too, the Prophet Mohammed had set the precedent, by demanding the young wife of his faithful follower, Ali, and, better still, obtaining her.

The *m'allim* said it was good doctrine that the willingness of Ali Higg to part with her constituted full divorce, and whether or not duress might have had anything to do with his consent made no difference. The lady's preferences having no kind of bearing on the case, Ayisha was not consulted.

But she was satisfied — no doubt of that. I think she admired Grim more than any man she had ever known; but tribal history was in her veins, as it is in every man's and woman's.

What she wanted was an influential husband, and she had one, for which she was as grateful to Grim as a stray cat for a saucer of milk. It was up to her to establish a position for herself among the senior wives, and by the look in her eye I should say she felt like doing it.

About four in the afternoon she asked leave of the Avenger to go and select the fifty men who were to constitute her dowry. Ali Higg demanded to go with her, to prevent her taking all the best; so Grim went too, and our whole party rode with Grim to prevent any last-minute treachery on the Lion's part.

It was a good job that we all went in the circumstances. There was a new arrival behind that sugar-loaf hill, and a real re-enforcement after all. Jael Higg, constitutionally restless, opportunist always, huntress with all hounds and runner with all hares in sight — everlastingly haunted, too, by doubt of Ali Higg's ability — had scraped together every last man Petra could produce, and brought them to the scene, trusting to her own sharp wit to use them to the best advantage. She had scraped together nearly fifty, including some women, but they were a rather bob-tailed lot and their camels were living skeletons.

Ali Higg tried to avoid her, but there wasn't much of the retiring arbutus about Jael. She tackled him in front of us all, and tongue-lashed him bitterly when she had dragged the story out of him, he trying in return to assert his overlordship, but with small success. The part that seemed to sting her most was the discovery that Grim had all along retained that order on the bank.

She advanced toward him with her thin lips quivering nervously, and cold hatred glaring from her eyes; and we all closed in, to prevent murder.

"So you kept that letter, did you? Clever, aren't you, Jimgrim! You've fooled me at every turn, haven't you? Proud, aren't you, to have me in money-hobbles for three years to come? Very well; you won this time, but wait and see!"

"I've left you lots to build with, Jael, if you'll only build to the line," he answered kindly.

"Left me lots — and fifty men and camels to go with that wandering gypsy Ayisha? Bah! You've skinned me to the bone. Ayisha may take these that I brought with me today."

But Ayisha was already choosing her contingent, and there was no reluctance to be chosen. Changing to the stronger side and a less irascible leader had its obvious advantages. Jael rushed off to interfere, and Ayisha cocked her rifle instantly.

Quick work by Ali Baba's men prevented that duel. Half a dozen of them pounced on Jael from behind and pinned her arms behind her, and the rest got in position to spoil Ayisha's aim. Ayisha threatened to shoot through them, but they laughed at her, and at a word from Grim she put her rifle up. Then Grim went and stood in front of Jael, but did not tell Ali Baba's men to let go her hands.

"See here, Jael, old girl," he said, "you're nervous and jumpy. You'll be doing something you'll regret if you don't watch points. Suppose you take that Lion of yours and your remaining men, and head straight back for Petra before you make your trouble any worse."

"Let me go, then."

"Say the word, Jimgrim, and we cut her throat," Ali Baba called out from behind.

Beyond holding his hand up as a signal for nothing doing, Grim did not answer. He walked up to Ali Higg instead, and ordered him to take his men away. The Lion obeyed readily enough; he was sick of the whole business, and desperately eager to get back into his cave, where he could growl himself into better spirits.

There was delay at the last minute, owing to the fact that many more than fifty men, including Ibrahim ben Ah, wanted to stay with Ayisha; but Ayisha had chosen her contingent and lined them up. Grim gave the rest thirty seconds to start after Ali Higg. He didn't say what the consequences would be if they refused; but there were a couple of hundred of the Avenger's men within hail, and they might imagine what they liked.

W HEN the last of the Lion's men was about two hundred yards away Grim ordered Jael released and her camel brought to her. Ali Baba wanted to keep her weapons, but Grim disallowed that. She mounted and rode away without a word of farewell, and Ali Baba croaked out his opinion that hornets' stings are usually in their tails. But Grim laughed.

Jael did turn once, at about two hundred yards' range, and threaten Grim with her rifle; but as every single one of Ali Baba's men promptly took aim at her she thought better of it.

"We've not had quite the last of that lady, I suspect; she still has one chance left, and overlooks no bets," said Grim.

That one chance was obviously to waylay us on our road home; and, seeing that Grim had added fifty to his force, the Avenger was kind enough to offer us an escort of a hundred men as far as the British frontier. But if Grim had agreed to that there would have been a fight in all likelihood, which in itself would constitute excuse for treating the signed agreement as a scrap of paper. If only one shot were fired by Jael's men, the Avenger would interpret that as breach of faith and act accordingly.

So Grim insisted on the treaty being carried out in full. We said good-by to the Avenger and Ayisha, and stood by at dusk to see the whole force file southward out of Abu Lissan.

The Avenger's last words as he shook Grim's hand were ominous:

"By Allah and the Prophet's body, Jimgrim, I shall hold thee to our terms! If no occasion rises to summon thee to my aid in a difficulty, may Allah change my face and roll me in the dust unless I make one!"

Ayisha didn't forget her obligations. She came and kissed Grim's hand, and gave him her amber necklace.

"If I have a new husband and am once more a princess, I am none the less beholden to thee for it," she said prettily.

And because Grim didn't know quite what to do about the necklace and was obviously embarrassed, Narayan Singh came to the rescue with one of his heavy-handed jests:

"By my teeth and the Prophet's belly!" he boomed impiously. "Princess thou mayest be; but I am a Pathan of the Orakzai! Let this be the Avenger's hour, and let him make the most of it; for as surely as the moon will shine tonight — as surely as thine eyes are worth a ransom — I will slay ninety and nine Avengers — aye! And burn Arabia for one more look into Ayisha's eyes!"

The Avenger overheard that, and felt rather flattered. He tossed back over his shoulder a mocking invitation to Narayan Singh to come and fight him single-handed for the girl at any time. So we all parted in a rare good temper, Ayisha having the last word, as a lady should.

"A Pathan is a pig, but thou art not so bad as some pigs!" she called back to Narayan Singh; and thereafter, all the way back home to El-Kalil, the gang kept chaffing him unmercifully about different breeds of pigs, pretending to wonder wherein he was so obviously different from the rest.

But that was because they knew he was a Sikh, and that the Sikhs don't object to pigs at all. If he had really been a Pathan those jokes would have cost a life or two.

We were a whole day longer on the road home than if we had taken the shortest way. Grim led us over a waterless route to the southward; and the proof of the wisdom of that was the sight we had of a party of camel-men, led almost certainly by Jael Higg, who reached a ravine too late to intercept us. For about an hour they followed in hot pursuit and then, giving up the chase, sat their camels on a ridge five miles away and watched us gloomily until we disappeared from view.

Spirits rose high after that; for the danger was all behind and El-Kalil in front, with the *suk* and the coffee-shops, where Ali Baba and his sons and grandsons could boast and lie to their hearts' content about our lawless doings.

Mahommed, the gang poet, rose to the occasion nobly with an epic song of our adventure; and being a poet, of course he wasn't hampered by any such trivialities as facts. If a story is worth singing, it is worth enlarging on; so he enlarged, to everybody's satisfaction. I remember a few stanzas; he sang the story part, composing as he went along, and we all thundered the refrain:

Saoud the Avenger —
   Sing of the Avenger! —
   Akbar the Avenger! —
Struck the earth in anger,
Swore an oath in anger.
Vowed before his captains
He will harry Ali Higg!
   Akbar the Avenger!
   Down with Ali Higg!

Saoud the Avenger —
   Sing of the Avenger!
   Akbar the Avenger! —
Summoned all his camel-men,
Made the desert dark with them;
Twenty-five machine-guns
Sent he in advance.
   Tap-ap-ap machine-guns
   Sent he in advance!

Half a hundred captains —
   Each he had a squadron;
   Half a hundred squadrons! —
Swore to do his bidding;
Allah bear them witness,
They will enter Petra,
The hold of Ali Higg!
   Burn and plunder Petra,
   The hold of Ali Higg!
   Akbar the Avenger! Akbar the Avenger!
   He shall eat up Petra,
   The abode of Ali Higg!

Lo! The Lion of Petra —
   Ha! the Lion of Petra!
   Ali Higg of Petra! —
Rose and cursed in answer
Swearing by the Prophet,
Father of a thousand boils,
Father of a rage!
   Wallah! Ya, the wrath of him!
   Roaring Ali Higg!

Summoned he Ayisha —
   Shellabi Ayisha [Beautiful Ayisha],
   Starry-eyed Ayisha! —
Bade her lead his camel-men
Straight at the Avenger,
Meet him at the desert wells,
Give him battle there!
   Shellabi Ayisha!
   Shellabi kabir! [Supremely beautiful!]

Called he his commander —
   Father of commanders,
   Fiercest of commanders! —
Gave him, too, a thousand
Princes of the desert,
Bade him and Ayisha
Bring him Saoud's head!
   Shellabi Ayisha!
   Ibrahim ben Ah!

It was a first-class song, with never an end to it, for Mahommed added stanza after stanza as the days wore by. It included finally a wonderful account of my defeat of Mujrim in the Valley of Moses, and Mujrim was made the hero of it by the ingenious process of ascribing fearful and supernatural qualities to me. But the whole song was merely a setting for the wholly fictitious story of Grim's conquest in battle of the allied "thousands" of the Avenger and Ali Higg combined, winding up with a gorgeous climax, in which Grim carried off "Shellabi Ayisha" from under the eyes of both of them. Grim was the hero of the epic, and however long the song grew by day, it always ended with a final crashing chorus:

Akbar! Akbar! Jimgrim! Jimgrim!

We sang it all the way home, and roared it in the narrow streets of El-Kalil; and although I suppose that Homer may have been more truthful, I've a notion he is an overrated epic-builder in comparison to my friend Mahommed ben Ali Baba ben Hamza, youngest son of Ali Baba, dean of thieves and wiliest old fox in Palestine.

Sing of Mahommed –
Ben Ali ben Hamza!

THE END

www.ingramcontent.com/pod-product-compliance
Lightning Source LLC
Chambersburg PA
CBHW020657180626
46816CB00003B/1328